"Look at me, my cold little wife!"

Diego's voice had developed an edge. "Only weeks ago you professed to love me, so how can you remain so cold? Why must I always take what a loving wife gives freely?"

Jade did look up then, shocked that Diego could take their moments of deep intimacy and use them as barbs to pierce the composure that was her only defense against him.

"I never loved you," she told him simply, ignoring his tightening grip. "I loved the tender, considerate man I imagined you to be. You charged me with deceit, but are you guiltless? 'Man is a moon with his dark side hidden,'" she quoted shakily. "And it would seem, Diego, that I'm condemned to live the rest of my life in your dark shadow!"

Miss High and Mighty

by

MARGARET ROME

Harlequin Books

TORONTO • LONDON • LOS ANGELES • AMSTERDAM
SYDNEY • HAMBURG • PARIS • STOCKHOLM • ATHENS • TOKYO

Original hardcover edition published in 1980
by Mills & Boon Limited

ISBN 0-373-02445-2

Harlequin edition published December 1981

CHAPTER ONE

'THINK of it, girls, just one more week to go until my holidays, five more working days until I say goodbye to custard creams and hello Torremolinos!'

A dozen heads lifted, a dozen backs straightened as the voice gloating upon pleasures to come penetrated the noise of machinery and reached to the far end of a conveyor belt laden with biscuits being gathered and stacked into tins by nimble-fingered packers.

'I've another month to wait,' a second girl sighed, 'but this year we're going to Majorca—my Ted's fed up with Torremolinos, he says it's all fish and chips and bingo.' Visibly she preened. 'As he says, "Majorca has a bit more class."'

Hoots of derisive laughter greeted this statement.

'Oh, my gawd!' one of her workmates spluttered. 'Can you imagine her Ted going all refined, demanding coq au vin for his supper instead of queueing at the chippy?'

'Packing up his job as a bingo caller and taking up chess!'

'Come off it, Kath,' a ribald challenge issued from the bottom end of the band, 'you know as well as we do that twenty-four hours after he arrives your Ted'll be so tanked up with booze he won't know whether he's in Majorca or Blackpool!'

Thoroughly squashed, the girl with genteel aspirations lapsed into a sulky silence. But the mood had been set, interest was aroused, and with only half an hour to go before a bell was due to ring signalling the end of a working week and the beginning of a weekend of freedom the girls felt loath to relinquish the subject until it had been squeezed dry of humour.

Jade's heart lurched, as she sensed the assessment of a pair of malevolent eyes.

'And what about you, Miss High and Mighty!' Jade shuddered from the jeer. 'Which exotic holiday spot are you deigning to favour?'

Suppressing a rise of colour, Jade managed a polite reply. 'I haven't decided yet.'

It was too much to hope for that Lynne, a girl who had shown instant and puzzling dislike at first meeting, would allow her the anonymity she sought—had always sought. As expected, she seized the opportunity to exercise her talent for mimicry.

'Oh, hark at that, girls! *"Aiy haven't decided yet!"'* she parodied, contorting her features into an expression of snooty disdain. 'It's so difficult, y'know, when you have to choose between the Canary Islands, the Bahamas, or the South of France!'

Jade braced to combat an expected spate of hurtful remarks, but for once the rest of her workmates seemed disinclined to follow Lynne's lead. Perhaps it was because of the stricken look Jade had not been quick enough to mask, or maybe it was a trembling bottom lip, hastily bitten, that gave rise to a suspicion that she was not half so composed as she tried to appear. Whichever it was, the result was an embarrassed silence and a hastily muttered:

'Give it a rest, Lynne, the kid can't help her la-di-da ways.'

'Yes, you do that, Lynne!' A hard, angry voice issued a challenge from across Jade's shoulder. 'Either that, or pick on somebody your own weight.'

Recognising the voice of her friend, Jade spun round to protest, 'I'm all right, Di, there's no need for you to become involved.' But her heart sank at the sight of Di's flashing eyes; her quick temper was aroused, even her red hair that clashed so incongruously against the pink of her chargehand's overall looked more vibrant than usual, activated by inner rage.

For a second Lynne seemed content to glower, then angered by her workmates' furtive sniggers, she accused, 'Pulling rank again to protect your pal? Why don't you leave her to fight her own battles instead of hovering like a mother hen around her chick? Why should she be singled out for special treatment, she's no better than the rest of us—and, pink overall or not, neither are you! In fact,' she hesitated before plunging boldly, 'it beats me why the pair of you have such high opinions of yourselves, considering your background. At least the rest of us,' she indicated her gaping-mouthed workmates with a nod, 'have families that care about us—unlike you two, we weren't dumped in an orphanage!'

A dozen pairs of appalled eyes fell upon Di who, though fighting to maintain the dignity expected of one in her position, looked ready to tear her flexing fingers through Lynne's straggling, blonde-streaked hair. Then to Jade's utter relief Di's hard core of common sense prevailed. Visibly she relaxed, then with a grin that infuriated Lynne far more than any loss of control would have done, she tilted lightly:

'Perhaps our conceit stems from the fact that having been deprived children we're determined never to allow ourselves to become deprived adults. Jade and I had no say in the matter when we were taken into care and brought up in a council home, but you, Lynne, live on a council estate from choice!'

'My husband is poorly paid,' Lynne flashed, incensed, 'on his wages we couldn't afford to live anywhere else!'

'And yet you married him.' Di's tone was mild, yet Jade knew from past observation that she was thoroughly enjoying herself.

'You ... you ... stuck-up orphanage brat!' Lynne's rage escalated. 'I suppose you and Miss High and Mighty here expect to do better!'

'But of course, doesn't everyone!' Di's tone contained a masterly degree of irony. A little more and she would have sounded venomous, a little less and all impact would have been lost. As it was, she left her listeners in no doubt of her contempt of Lynne's life-style.

'Some of us put love before money,' a workmate championed Lynne.

'And others are sensible enough to love where money is,' Di countered sweetly.

'You mean you've both decided to marry for money?' Lynne hooted. 'In that case, you'd better leave your jobs, or resign yourselves to becoming old maids, for you'll never find rich husbands in a factory!'

There was a concerted sigh of relief when the flood of biscuits began petering into a trickle and the girls were able to disband and prepare themselves for the rush towards the exit the moment the bell of freedom sounded.

Jade was last in line to punch her clock card and as Di was often delayed by last-minute problems she waited so that they could walk home together. As she dallied, she pondered about the flat they shared. When, after five years of living in digs, they had decided to pool their incomes and invest in a home of their own, Jade had been prepared to aim her sights low—but not Di.

'As this will probably be the most important investment we shall ever make in our lives let's make the effort worthwhile,' she had urged, dismissing Jade's conservative choice of a rather run-down area with a tilt of her upturned nose. 'This is what we want!' She had jabbed a finger, indicating an advertisement in the local paper.

Wide-eyed, Jade had read: Luxury flat to let. Two bedrooms; spacious lounge; fitted kitchen; central heating throughout; garage and small garden plot.

'We can't afford that!' she had gasped. 'And anyway, what would we want with a garage?'

'We *can* afford it.' With a singlemindedness that was typical of her, Di had brushed Jade's argument aside. 'I've worked it all out—my promotion has come at exactly the right time, with the extra money we can just manage to offer the rent being asked. As for the garage,' she had shrugged, 'perhaps we could sub-let it, or better still, once we've found our feet, we might buy a second-hand car.'

'But ... but the flat is on the Scaur!' Jade had stressed.

'So what?' Stubbornly Di had refused to admit the incongruity of two factory girls aspiring to live in the most exclusive area of town. 'Our money's as good as the next person's.'

'Yes, but ...' cautious of Di's prickly pride, Jade had trodden gently, 'perhaps the owner won't consider us suitable—after all, he'll probably feel duty-bound not to upset the occupiers of the adjoining flats who, in all probability, will be extremely ... er ... snobbish.'

'Which is why all the negotiations must be conducted by you,' Di had grinned. 'Even if he shouldn't prove susceptible to a pretty face there's no way he could find fault with either your manners or your accent. For once,' she had sighed blissfully, 'instead of being a drawback, your air of refinement might prove to be an asset.'

She had, as usual, been proved right.

When Di finally appeared, pulling on her coat as she ran towards her, Jade subconsciously noted, as she had for days past, that her friend's air of vivacity seemed forced. Outwardly, she looked as cheerful as ever, her smile as ready, her quips lacking none of their sting, yet Jade's intuitive senses were alerted by the fact that lately Di's humour had not quite reached her eyes and that, on occasions when she thought herself unobserved, her brow became furrowed by deep worry lines. She had resisted the impulse to pry, not because she feared Di's fiery temper, but because she knew that she would confide her worries only when she was ready.

Yet in spite of her insight into her friend's impetuous nature, she was shocked when, after leaving the factory and hurrying in the direction of a nearby shopping centre, Di burst out:

'Let's indulge ourselves for once! How about buying steak for supper ... and salad ... and a bottle of wine?'

Jade's eyes widened. 'Steak is horribly expensive! And as for wine—what do we have to celebrate?'

'We're young, healthy, and comparatively happy, aren't we?' Di snapped so irritably Jade decided it would be politic to humour her.

'Of course we are,' she smiled, soothing Di's guilty conscience with a smile. 'Which kind of steak do you prefer, rump or fillet?'

Di opted for fillet, thick, succulent-looking steaks at a price that caused Jade a pained wince. Then they bought salad stuff, a long stick of crusty French bread, and giggled for ten minutes over a choice of wine from the supermarket shelves.

Encouraged by a sweet tooth, Di plumped for Asti, but Jade shuddered and shook her head. 'I'm not spoiling my meal by drinking *that*!' Di objected, seeing Jade's hand hovering over a bottle of Moselle.

'Oh, very well,' Jade sighed, 'we'll compromise and settle for Mateus Rosé.'

With Di's humour completely restored they happily began trudging the two-mile journey home, an exercise undertaken twice daily, hail, rain, or snow, ostensibly to keep their figures trim but mainly because the cost of bus fares played havoc with their budget.

'By the way,' Jade panted as they struggled up the hill leading to the elevated Scaur, 'are you going out with Gordon tonight?'

Di's carefree look fled. 'No, not tonight,' she replied abruptly. 'I thought, after supper, you might wash and set my hair.'

'Of course I will.' Jade's tone was traced through with surprise. 'But you always go out with Gordon on Friday evening, so why?'

'Just for the hell of it, I'm staying in tonight!' Di twisted round to glare. 'Nothing bores me more than repetition, doing the same things, in the same way, on the same day of each week! Don't *you* ever feel like throwing your cap over the windmill instead of floundering in a rut, doing everything that's expected of you, living as if each day were numbered—day one, see Gordon; day two, go to Judo classes; day three, clean the flat . . .'

She was still muttering a string of resentments when she pushed the key into the lock of their front door, pushed it open, and headed straight for the kitchen, overlooking, in her haste, a letter lying in the hallway.

Jade picked it up from the carpet and laid it on the table, her eyes too troubled, too unseeing, to register any more than that the envelope looked rather official. She felt cold and somehow threatened. Di had always been of a volatile nature, up one day, down the next, but never before had she betrayed such deep frustration, such resentment of their routine Jade herself enjoyed and which, up until now, she had considered ideal.

Anxious and uncertain, she followed into the kitchen where, amazingly, Di swung from the sink to flash her a wide grin.

'I'll prepare the salad while you grill the steaks,' airily she waved a lettuce leaf in the direction of the fridge, 'and it might be as well if you put the wine in there to chill!'

Jade sighed and proceeded to carry out her instructions. With the speed of light Di's mood had once more changed; no amount of digging would extract further information, so she knew she would have to wait for yet another reversal.

'Why was that cat Lynne getting at you again today?' Di queried, sounding determined to keep their conversation light and impersonal.

'Lynne ...? Oh, I'm not sure.' Jade had difficulty in dragging her mind back to the subject of her workmate. 'Her attitude has always been unfriendly, for some unknown reason she registered dislike from our first moment of meeting.'

Di chuckled. 'Well, you did get everyone's back up rather.'

'I did? How ...?'

'Don't you remember?' Di looked round, her eyebrows elevating. 'No, I don't suppose you do.' her exasperated sigh caused Jade even more bewilderment, 'being precise and formal comes as naturally to you as breathing. Yet you can hardly blame the girls for thinking they were being patronised when a slip of a girl, straight out of school, replies to a friendly enquiry: "My name is Miss Jade Iris Mighty" in such a cool, polite manner they immediately felt they were being warned not to take liberties. It was hardly surprising,' she concluded dryly, 'that our quick-witted workmates should promptly dub you "Miss High and Mighty".'

'Which was most unfair,' Jade objected with rising colour. 'I was merely introducing myself in the manner in which I'd been taught.'

'*I* know that,' Di cheerfully agreed, 'but they didn't, so far as they were concerned you were trying to be different—and different, in the eyes of someone like Lynne, means stuck up!'

Rapidly Jade blinked back tears and strove for composure as she set two places on a table covered by a gay chequered cloth. 'For four years I've tried hard to become accepted, but still the girls treat me as an outsider. I seem to be stuck with that hateful nickname.'

'Never mind,' Di consoled, plonking a bowl of salad in the middle of the table, 'it's not your fault. Your mother didn't do you any favours when she opted for sending you to a private school and keeping you isolated from potential friends by insisting that all your spare time should be spent in her beauty salon.'

The salad looked crisp and colourful, the steaks were done to a turn, yet Jade's appetite fled at the mention of her mother, who had constituted all the family she had ever known. Swallowing hard to disperse a lump in her throat, she defended stiffly:

'Mother's illness came upon her without warning, she'd never suffered a day's illness in her life, so how could she have been expected to foresee an early death?'

With a dismayed gasp Di put down her fork. 'I didn't mean to sound critical——'

'No,' Jade interrupted, 'you were implying, as others have implied before you, that it was selfish and inconsiderate of her not to have made provision for my future. Nothing could have been further from the truth,' she insisted fiercely. 'It couldn't have been easy for her, bringing up a child on her own and trying to build up a successful business at the same time. If she had one fault, it was that she was too ambitious for my future. Everything my mother did, everything she planned, was aimed at providing me with a life better than her own. She spent next to nothing on herself, most of the profits from the salon went on school fees, private tuition in dancing, deportment, tennis and horse riding, and what little time she had to spare was spent teaching me the art of a beautician. Her one goal in life was to turn me into a lady—thank God,' Jade choked, 'she died without knowing that her daughter had been taken into care.'

Di pushed aside her plate, leaving the meal so eagerly anticipated almost untouched. Jade, exercising her flair for setting the perfect atmosphere, had arranged a centrepiece of flowers around a solitary red candle left over from Christmas, and as Di eyed her friend across its glittering wick she felt a surge of impotent anger, of regret, and of sadness that such beauty should be left to waste. Even without the benefit of her mother's teaching, Jade's charms were undeniable, but emphasised with the skill of an artist's brush, her small heart-shaped face had a loveliness that was breathtaking— delicately arched brows darkened finely as a feather; luxuriant lashes tipped with gold; a mist of green shadow breathed across downcast lids; skin pale and pure as cream; soft, full lips, pink and trembling as butterflies' wings.

'Sorry I was so tactless,' Di cleared her throat and

peered anxiously at Jade's downbent head. 'It was not my intention to revive hurtful memories,'

When Jade looked up and swept a swathe of lint-fair hair from across her face forgiveness was radiating from the depths of her dark green eyes.

'You're forgiven,' she flashed a half-troubled, half-teasing smile, 'on one condition.'

'And that is ...?' Di prompted.

'That you stop snapping at me like a terrier and come right out with whatever it is that's troubling you!'

For a second Di looked mutinous, but after a pause for thought her stubborn mouth twisted into a wry, humourless grin.

'I've never been able to hide anything from you, Jade, I don't know why I even bother to try.' Egged on by Jade's encouraging smile, she blurted, 'It's Gordon ...'

'You've fallen out again!' Relief washed to Jade's very fingertips. 'But you do that regularly, at least once a week, then you just as regularly make up again.'

But Di seemed unable to meet her eyes. She turned her head aside, and as she did so candle-glow brushed against her lashes, highlighting a glint of hidden tears. Jade caught a sharp breath. Di had never been known to cry, in the orphanage her stoicism had been pointed out as an example to others; amongst her fellow orphans she had been revered as a real 'tough nut'. Obviously, something dreadful must have happened.

As if ashamed of showing weakness, Di blinked rapidly, then launched into an explanation with a brisk show of aloofness that did not fool Jade for one minute.

'This time it's not that simple—I'm afraid the gulf between myself and Gordon is too great ever to be breached. He's been offered promotion—it's no more than he deserves, because he's ambitious and has studied hard—however, the bank insists that he must move to a branch in another town, and the conceited idiot imagined that I'd be prepared to marry him immediately so that I could go with him when he moved. He even had the audacity,' she choked, 'to wave a special licence under my nose.'

Long afterwards, Jade was able to pinpoint that moment as a time of instant maturity. She had never considered herself to be particularly quick-witted, cunning, or expert in artifice, but one blinding flash of insight enabled her to become immediately proficient in all three. Only one thing was preventing Di from marrying the man she loved—not injured pride, as she had tried to imply, nor regret at leaving a job she hated, but loyalty to a friend who she imagined was too timid and insecure to cope on her own.

'Oh, that is a pity!' Jade could hardly believe that the cool, nonchalant voice was her own. 'If you turn down Gordon it will mean that my own plans will have to be revised.'

'Your plans ...?' Di's hushed whisper was proof, if any were needed, that her motives had been assessed correctly.

'Yes.' With just sufficient regret to make her words sound like a confession Jade continued to amaze herself. 'Thinking, mistakenly as it turns out, that you and Gordon were bound to be considering marriage sooner or later I felt justified in laying plans for my own future. You see, Di,' she edged out of range of telltale candlelight and willed her voice to remain steady, 'I decided some time ago that I was not cut out to be a factory worker. I also felt I was being disloyal to my mother by not making use of the skills she taught me, so, realising that I still have much to learn about the beauty business, I began making enquiries about finishing my training and was fortunate enough to make contact with an old colleague of my mother's who offered me a job in his London salon.'

'And you meant to turn it down because of me?' Di became so excited she began to babble. 'Oh, no, Jade, you mustn't ... there's no need ... I want to marry Gordon, truly I do!' Laughing with delight, she rushed from the table to throw her arms around Jade. 'Oh, Jade, isn't life *marvellous*, isn't it simply wonderful when dreams start to come true?'

CHAPTER TWO

As the wing of the plane tipped sideways Jade looked down and glimpsed far below the roofs and spires of the city of Lisbon sprawling across low hills sloping gently towards the wide, sparkling blue River Tagus. Portugal! She gulped, wondering how many people would allow themselves to be guided in the choice of a holiday resort by the label on a wine bottle—as she had!

In a terrified sort of trance she sat watching the ground rising up to meet her. In five more minutes the plane was due to land, then for the first time in her life she would step on to foreign soil, become cast adrift from even her fellow passengers who, though complete strangers, could at least speak her own language.

Why had she allowed herself to succumb to the sudden insane impulse to venture abroad? Granted, she had been forced to remove herself from Di's vicinity, to cut completely the bond of dependence between them, but she could have managed that equally well within the British Isles, instead of fleeing to a land which, according to the travel brochures, abounded with vineyards, corkwoods, *quintas* and Moorish castles.

It had been her win that had prompted the reckless move. Hours after her sort-out with Di, after wedding plans had been discussed, a date set, she had remembered the letter left on the table in the

hallway. With her mind still buzzing, her heart cold
with fear at the prospect of a solitary future, she
had ripped open the envelope and stared at the
jumble of words and figures with uncomprehend-
ing eyes.

'Di,' she had appealed, 'what does this mean?'

Di had glanced across her shoulder. '*Jade!*' she
had yelled in her excitement. 'That premium bond
you bought, *it's come up* ... you've won five thousand pounds!'

Many times since her mother had died Jade had
prayed for deliverance from situations that had
appeared intolerable, but this time, without being
given time to pray, help had arrived just when it
was needed in the shape of sufficient money to buy
Di and Gordon the sort of wedding present they
deserved, sufficient to replenish her repleted wardrobe; to make it easy to give up her job, and finally
to take the most tremendous step of all, that of
spending a holiday abroad before deciding where
she should live, where to begin her life anew.

'*Passaporte, senhorita, por favor.*'

'What ...?' Jade's dazed eyes steadied and a uni-
formed official swam into view.

The plane had landed and without conscious
volition she had been swept along with her fellow
passengers towards the Customs hall.

'Oh, yes ... just a second ...' Panic-stricken by
the official's dark frown, she began rummaging in
her handbag.

'Take as long as you like, *senhorita,* I am last in
the queue and I don't mind waiting.' The amused
masculine voice was projected across her shoulder.
Startled, she swung round, and somehow the bag

slipped from her nerveless fingers, its contents scattering around the stranger's feet.

'Oh, *no* ...!' she gasped, diving to rescue her belongings.

The stranger also swooped and with perfect timing both heads, one lint-fair, one raven black, collided in mid-air. Intense pain jabbed rapier-sharp across Jade's brow, a myriad stars danced in front of her eyes. As she staggered backwards a hand grabbed her arm and as if from miles away she heard a sharp, unmistakable curse followed immediately by strange words muttered in a tone of abject apology.

'*Sinto nuito. Que pena!* I'm terribly sorry, *menina!*'

When the fierce pain had ebbed a little Jade opened her eyes to stare into the face of the man bending over her, then for long bewildering seconds her senses floundered as she felt drowned in the depths of eyes more intensely blue than any she had ever previously seen. A whispered gasp escaped her lips as she weathered the impact, unable to move, unable to speak, in the presence of a man impeccably dressed in a lightweight suit mere shades darker than an expensive silk shirt set off by a quietly-patterned tie, yet whose hands had the grip of whipcord, whose skin, moulded across flared nostrils, high cheekbones, and a lean sweep of jaw, was tanned and supple as leather.

'He looks,' she thought, staring wide-eyed and speechless, 'as I imagine a brigand would look or a Bedouin—one of the aristocrats of the desert who use the wilderness as a pillow and are so completely assured they need only the stars for company.'

'You seem dazed, *senhorita,* are you all right?' Strangely, he sounded as shaken as she felt, which was as if the earth had exploded, whirling her through the universe before depositing her at the feet of a fascinating inhabitant of some strange, unknown planet.

'Call a taxi!' she heard him rap. 'Then find out from the labels on her luggage at which hotel the *senhorita* is staying.'

Seconds later she was airborne, lifted from the ground into a pair of strong arms that carried her without effort through a gaping crowd then outside the airport to where a taxi was waiting.

'Hotel Grande Vastelo!' he instructed the driver, who flung open the rear door, then hovered anxiously until she had been settled in the rear seat of the taxi. 'Don't worry about your luggage, *senhorita,*' her dark protector assured her, 'it is being sent direct to your hotel. My immediate concern is that you receive the attention of a doctor.'

Jade's common sense rose to the surface. 'No, really, *senhor,* there is no need, I'm feeling better already. I'm sorry to have caused you so much trouble, I ... I ...' she stumbled, then blushed, wondering what his reaction would be if she should try to explain that she was suffering not so much from a crack on the head as from the impact of his compelling personality. 'I was dazed for a while, but I'm perfectly all right now.'

She was almost made to eat her words when he smiled, a flash of white teeth against bronzed skin that started a leap of excitement into her throbbing pulses.

'I'm so relieved to hear you say so.' He reached out to enclose her shaking hands within lean brown fingers. 'I curse myself for my clumsiness,' he murmured, seductive as a bee droning expectantly around the heart of a flower, 'yet I must confess to feeling grateful for the opportunity of becoming acquainted, even though the manner of our introduction was slightly unusual.'

Jade sensed tender amusement in his tone, but kept her eyes fastened upon his signet ring, a heavy gold band clasped around a sinewed middle finger with, chased upon its surface, an emblem of nature, a slender, newly-born crescent moon. Her heart was thumping so loudly she had to strain to hear honeyed words spoken with a sincerity that robbed them entirely of offence.

'I sat opposite you in the plane,' he admitted softly. 'You looked so lonely and afraid that many times I had to restrain an impulse to speak to you, to offer my help, or simply to chat your fears away; but you were so deep in thought intrusion would have been impertinent. Even when we landed, you stepped from the plane as if in a walking dream, which is why I took it upon myself to act as your shadow and to intervene when you seemed in need of protection. Am I forgiven, *senhorita*?' he urged gently. 'Amongst my own people, it would be considered unforgivable for a man to press his attentions upon a solitary girl, but then no Portuguese girl of your tender years would ever be permitted to travel alone.'

'So you are Portuguese ...' Jade responded in a breathless rush.

'I am.' He inclined his head. 'My name is Diego da Luz Pereira da Silves, but please call me Diego.

And what, sweet English Miss, am I to call you?'

'My name is ...' Just in time she remembered the effect her last prim introduction had had upon her workmates '... Jade will do,' she continued hurriedly. 'Miss Mighty sounds so formal.'

'And so wrong,' his lips twitched. 'Mighty implies power—you, *minha cara,* possess the power of a petal floating on a breeze.' He raised her hand to his lips, confusing her utterly, then lightly kissed each fingertip in turn. His head inclined nearer, then hesitated mere inches from her young, vulnerable mouth. 'Jade, because of the colour of your beautiful eyes, of course,' he murmured on a breath, 'but in my own mind I christened you hours ago. *Princesa de Neze*—always, you will appear to me as a lovely snow princess.'

Immediately the taxi drew to a halt in front of the hotel his manner changed. Politely, but showing strict formality, he helped her out of the taxi, then guided her with a light touch upon her elbow through the foyer and towards the reception desk.

'Kindly escort Senhorita Mighty to her room,' he instructed the clerk, 'then ensure that she is not disturbed for at least a couple of hours. She is in need of rest and quiet.'

Once the clerk had been galvanised into action, he turned to Jade to proffer a stiff bow. 'I, too, am a guest at this hotel, together wih my mother and my young sister Jacinta. Would you do us the honour of dining with us this evening?'

He spoke coolly, keeping his face expressionless, but Jade felt the impact of brilliant eyes urging her to accept the invitaion she had no will to resist.

'Th-thank you,' she stammered, a blush spreading a stain of pink under her creamy skin, 'I should like that very much.'

'Then *boa tarde, Princesa de Neze,*' he glinted secretly, 'until this evening.'

Jade floated in the wake of a porter sent to escort her to her room, feeling her feet were inches above ground as she followed him into a lift, along a passageway, then inside the room whose doors he opened wide. She tipped him hurriedly, then closed the door, anxious to be alone to savour to the utmost the thrill of her encounter with a charming stranger, a man of obvious wealth, of pride, of unconscious arrogance and, as his name had indicated, one of the aristocracy, a true Portuguese *fidalgo.*

Bemused by the effect his virile attractions had had upon her senses, she relaxed on to the bed and stared, starry-eyed, around the room.

'Bless you, Di,' she murmured, 'for persuading me that the extravagance of a five-star hotel was justified! Whatever the future might have in store, for the rest of my life I'll have this to remember— two weeks of luxury, a short, illicit escape into a completely different world. How you would love this room!' Slowly her drowsy eyes evaluated her surroundings—fitted wardrobes with sliding doors of light, honey-coloured wood; a matching dressing table tailored to fit neatly into the angle of two walls; the polished shine on a floor tiled for ultimate coolness; the telephone on the bedside cabinet partnered by a folder with an imposing crest upon its cover containing details of the many services available to guests day and night, together with a list of the appropriate numbers to ring; french windows standing slightly open, permitting a breeze to play amongst folds of net curtains screening a balcony furnished with chairs and a wrought iron table, where, she had already decided, she would enjoy a long, leisurely breakfast each morning. 'Sinful luxury!' She yawned and snuggled deeper into her pillow. 'I think perhaps the plane has taken me straight to heaven and forgotten to bring me down!' Not surprisingly, considering the traumatic past few days, she fell into a deep sleep, dreamless, yet filled with a contentment that curled her mouth into a smile as she slept.

Two hours had passed when a discreet tap upon the door startled her awake.

'Just a minute!' she panicked, then remembering where she was, she scrabbled in her mind for a response she had memorised from a phrase book. *'Entre, por favor!'*

As she was swinging her feet to the floor the door opened and a maid entered, preceding a porter laden with luggage.

'Boa tarde, senhorita!' Proffering a tray holding a gift-wrapped package, she stumbled slowly: 'I have been asked to give you this. Would the *senhorita* like me to unpack now?'

Jade was studying the package she had taken from the tray, wondering what it could possibly be, and was momentarily unaware that the girl was waiting for an answer. When realisation dawned, she blushed and declined hastily: 'No, thank you, I can manage by myself.'

When the girl's eyebrows rose, Jade realised her mistake. Before leaving home she had read as many books as she could find in the public library about the land she was about to visit and one of them had been less than complimentary about the nature of the upper class, and especially those living in Lisbon. *Most of them consider it beneath their dignity to carry packages or to do menial work of any description.*

With burning cheeks Jade rummaged in her handbag for a tip sizeable enough to allay the disdain of the maid and the hovering porter, then trying hard to appear dignified she dismissed them both. When the door closed behind them she sank back on to the bed, depressed by her obvious inadequacies. How had she dared to aspire to dining with an aristocrat and his no doubt formidable family when she was incapable of deceiving even members of the hotel staff? Upon closer acquaintance, Diego da Silves would be certain to conclude that she was out of her class—she would telephone the desk and ask them to convey apologies for her absence, for to dine with him and his family would be merely to invite humiliation.

While she was pondering, her fingers fretted through the bows of coloured ribbon decorating the parcel. As the knot gave way the wrapping paper slid apart, revealing a box with a cellophane lid enclosing a base of jade-green silk with, nestling upon its surface, one perfect snow-white rose. For a long time she sat motionless staring at the gift, then with shaking fingers she withdrew from its envelope a card covered with flowing script, black, forceful, outstanding as the writer himself. Slowly she read.

Words cannot describe my loneliness. Please look upon this flower as a plea from a hasty heart and if its message pleases you, Snow Princess, tell me so

*by wearing the rose this evening. May the hours
sprout wings. Yours, Diego.*

The card dropped from her fingers and landed,
writing uppermost, upon the floor from where the
bold, black symbols seemed to mock her naïveté,
her breathless, startled confusion.

What was the message he was trying to convey?
Was he at heart a philanderer or—she caught a
painful, sobbing breath—was he, too, reeling from
the impact of a world gone suddenly haywire, of
pounding nerves, tingling senses, and an urgent, in-
definable desire that had leapt into life the moment
their eyes had met? Could love strike like lightning, fusing two hearts as one in a blinding flash?
Was it possible for strangers to meet, to look, then
to fall immediately under one another's spell?

She did not know, and there was no one to advise her, but of one thing she was certain, she *had*
to look once more into Tagus-blue eyes, to wear his
rose, to trust in his sincerity and, if instinct should
be proved wrong, to hope that the devil would at
least be merciful . . .

As she luxuriated in a bath the colour of deep
blue sea surrounded by matching tiles dotted
occasionally with colourful fishes of some unnameable species, she could have found it easy to imagine
herself enclosed in an underground grotto had her
mind not been feverishly occupied with the problem of which dress she should wear that evening.

'*With an adequate wardrobe,*' her mother had
often maintained, '*you could take your place in
high society with as much ease as one born into it.*'

But Jade was not so sure. She had followed her
mother's instructions to the letter by investing in

well-cut, starkly simple basics and splurging extravagantly on accessories such as pure silk scarves; belts, handbags and shoes of genuine suede and leather. Two evening dresses would be sufficient, she had decided, to see her through solitary evenings during which she expected to dine alone and then retire immediately to her bedroom.

But Di had coaxed: 'Take at least a couple more! And don't dare go running off to your room the moment you finish your meal—if this investment is to pay off you must be prepared to hang around, using your assets as bait to trap the biggest fish available.'

Some of the shock Di's words had aroused still lingered. 'I wouldn't dream of doing such a thing!' Jade had gasped. 'Nor do I believe you're half so mercenary as you pretend—I wouldn't describe Gordon as wealthy, yet you seem quite happy to be marrying him.'

'You're right, he isn't wealthy,' Di had nodded agreement, 'but with his ambition and drive we'll never be less than comfortable.'

'You'd marry him whatever his prospects!' Jade had scoffed, only to have her confidence shattered by Di's quietly determined reply.

'No, I would not. You've never really taken seriously my vow not to marry a poor man, have you, Jade? But then, unlike me, you haven't known a lifetime of poverty and rejection. Oh, yes, I know you've had your share,' she had waved a dissenting hand when Jade had attempted to interrupt, 'but up until you were fourteen you had a mother to pamper and cosset you, whereas I was rejected at birth, so I never knew what it was like to live in a proper home or to wear clothes bought especially for me, instead of hand-me-downs outgrown by some other unfortunate. Okay,' her chin had jutted defiantly, 'so your sensitive soul is revolted at the idea of putting a price on love, but if you're sensible and start to face facts you'll realise that we live in a harsh, uncaring world and that if you hope to become a survivor you must begin by reversing your opinion and deciding to follow my example.'

Thoughtfully, Jade slid out of the rapidly-cooling bath water and drew a fluffy towel around silken-skinned limbs, fragrant with the perfume of spring-fresh lilac. There was no way she could subscribe to Di's views, yet an inner voice was beguiling: 'Surely no harm can come from enjoying the attentions of an attractive man when the association is destined to last no longer than two short weeks? It will be an interlude to look back upon, a memorable oasis to sustain you during a lifetime that promises to be as arid and lonely as any desert. You have nothing to lose providing you don't seek to gain!'

With trembling fingers she plucked confining pins from her hair and as the pale silken mass fell around her shoulders she glimpsed her own pale, frightened face reflected upon the surface of a steamy mirror. 'Scared, timid rabbit!' she glared, daring her resolution to falter, 'Diego da Silves is a gentleman—kind, thoughtful, scrupulously correct in his attitude towards what I'm certain he regards as the weaker sex—fool, to even suspect that he might be a wolf preparing to gobble you up for dinner!'

CHAPTER THREE

Two hours later Jade approached the imposing staircase leading down into the main foyer, feeling her quaking heart had sunk to somewhere within the region of her spindle-heeled, silver-strapped sandals.

At the head of the staircase she halted, overwhelmed by an urge to flee back into her room rather than intrude upon the throng of assured, expensively-dressed people milling down below. She placed pressure on one foot, ready to twirl around, then her frightened eyes were caught and held by a compelling blue stare being directed by Diego da Silves, who was waiting, suave and darkly handsome, at the foot of the staircase. Drawn by a compulsion that reduced her concrete will to jelly, she floated, one step at a time, towards the man whose brilliant eyes, slightly crooked smile, hawk-sharp features and tough, sinewed hands seemed to have taken complete control of her destiny.

At the foot of the stairs they drew close and though Diego's hands remained motionless she imagined she could feel their pressure enfolding her, and sensed from the intensity of his stare upon her quivering mouth that he was sharing her intense longing to kiss, and be kissed. After a pause that seemed an eternity, he broke the spell by reaching out for her hand and lifting it to his lips. As his mouth feathered across her fingertips she trembled.

He smiled, then assured her in a voice of roughened velvet:

'Your skin has the fragrance of an English spring-time, *cara*.' For propriety's sake he remained at a respectful distance, yet in spirit they could not have been closer, so close that he merely needed to whisper for his words to reach her acutely attuned ears. 'All afternoon I have been telling myself that my imagination was playing me tricks, that no one could be as beautiful as the image I carried around with me, that in this modern age it was not possible for any girl to remain so unworldly, so sweet, so full of touching innocence. I schooled myself for disappointment, certain in my mind that hair as fair as I remembered must be a myth conjured by dazzling sunlight, that eyes could achieve the colour of jade only by some trick of shifting shadow, that such texture of skin, such grace of movement was an impossible dream. Yet here you are, Snow Princess, living proof that my suspicions were unfounded.'

Jade's choked gasp, her look of panic, seemed to bring him to his senses. A shadow darkened his eyes, rendering them dark pools of secrecy, and as his shoulders squared he released her hand so that once again she experienced the same sense of desolation she had felt after her mother's death.

'Forgive me if I frightened you, *cara*,' he looked grave. 'My mother will tell you that impatience is one of my greatest failings—whatever I want, I want immediately, and waiting is an unendurable agony. But come,' his sudden grin caused a vulnerable nerve to jump, 'once you have met my family I will be spared the need to outline my many faults—

my mother and sister will delight in doing a more honest and thorough analysis.'

As he escorted her through a crowd of fellow guests enjoying aperitifs before going in to dinner she drew in a deep, steadying breath and urged herself to relax so that she might appear as confident as those around her. She knew that her appearance would not let her down; her plain white, slim-fitting dress had looked nothing hanging on the rack in the dress shop, which probably explained why it had so often been passed over and reduced in price so many times that it had eventually come within reach of her purse. But immediately she had slipped into it it had seemed to become part of her, charmed into chic elegance as it folded lovingly around voluptuously curved breasts, a waistline that masculine hands would find easy to span, then down a slender line of hip and thigh until the hem rested upon the delicate arch of small, neatly-tapering feet.

Because she had considered the plunging neck-line a little too revealing, she had tucked Diego's rose into the hollow of mystique formed by creamy breasts and thrown across her shoulders the gauzy cape embroidered with silver thread into a likeness of a glistening, dew-hung spider's web that had been her most wicked extravagance. Only inexperience and awkward shyness would give her away, she thought nervously, as Diego guided her in the direction of two women who were seated at a table watching with interest her progress across the room.

Repressing an inner quivering that was threatening to upset her composure, she halted at Diego's side and forced her stiff lips into a smile whilst he introduced her.

'Mae,' he addressed the elder woman whose severe black dress was relieved only slightly by a brooch set with fine diamonds, 'I'd like you to meet Jade—Senhorita Mighty—the English girl I told you about who became a victim of my clumsiness immediately she arrived in Portugal. Jade,' he drew her forward, 'this is my mother, Dona Amelia da Luz Pereira da Silves, who I am certain will want to atone for her son's behaviour by insisting that you address her informally as Dona Amelia.'

Jade told herself that she was overreacting when she imagined she heard a thread of steel running through his words, but the suspicion that his mother was not overjoyed to meet her was confirmed by her forced smile and limp, unenthusiastic handshake.

'And this young lady,' Diego jerked impatiently away from his mother, 'is my young sister, Jacinta, who at great length and speaking many untruths will tell you everything there is to know about me.'

Jade's relief was enormous when her diffident smile was returned by an ear-splitting grin from a dark, merry-eyed girl whom she judged to be about three years younger than herself.

'I have been so curious to meet you, Jade,' she gurgled, dispensing promptly with protocol, 'never have I known my brother so eager to renew an acquaintance! Throughout the length and breadth of Portugal he has been pursued by ambitious mothers and designing females, but he has persistently evaded them all. What is your secret, I wonder?' She cocked her head on one side, pretending to study Jade's embarrassed face. 'You are very lovely, of course, but then Diego has suffered a surfeit of beautiful women. You are extremely fair, but again, such colouring is not as unusual as a stranger might imagine in a land which for centuries was occupied by a race of fair-haired Moors almost Nordic in appearance, who, through intermarriage with Portuguese, combined to create an extraordinary mélange of peoples, customs, and physical characteristics—as evidenced,' she nodded towards Diego, 'by my brother's unusual blue eyes. No,' she considered impishly, 'I think it must be your English aloofness he finds so interesting—the cool, touch-me-not aura that clings to you must attract him as a moth is attracted to flame.'

'And to consequent destruction!' Dona Amelia snapped, incensed by the turn the conversation had taken.

'You forget yourselves, both of you!' This time there was no mistaking the ice encrusting Diego's tone. Jade's startled eyes flew to his face and saw an astonishingly rigid line of jaw, lips thinned by anger, and eyes that had developed a diamond-hard glint she found frightening. His attitude was austere, very much that of a proud *fidalgo* whose sense of propriety has been outraged. Stiffly he begged:

'Please excuse my mother's momentary impoliteness. Travelling tires her; she has not had time to recover from her journey, therefore she is feeling less conscious of her duties than one might otherwise expect. And as for my sister,' Jacinta seemed to shrivel when his eyes slewed her way, 'for many months she has been trying to persuade me that she is mature enough to join her friends in their latest fad—playing at running a boutique here in Lisbon. My doubts have now been justified by a display of rude outspokenness that is unforgivable.'

Losing all interest in his sister, he turned his brilliant eyes upon Jade, who watched, fascinated, as ice slowly thawed, revealing pools of tender blue. 'Forgive our family squabble,' he urged gently. 'If you have been made to feel unwelcome, dismiss the notion, for nothing could be further from the truth.'

She felt slight sympathy for Dona Amelia when, in an obvious attempt to soothe her son's outraged dignity, she swallowed her pride far enough to second: 'Yes, please do forgive our unfortunate lapse, *senhorita*. Come, sit by me, and while Diego is fetching you a drink you can tell me all about yourself.'

When she patted a space at her side with an imperiousness very much at odds with her tone of conciliation Jade's timidity forced her to obey what amounted to a command.

Diego's face darkened, but then with a shrug, half impatience, half masculine despair, he bolstered Jade's spirits with a smile before enquiring, 'What would you like to drink?'

Her mind froze. Doubtless, had she been given sufficient time, her mother would have filled in the gap in her education; as it was, however, she had no idea which drinks were considered suitable aperitifs. Then she recalled the bottle of wine she and Di had bought at the supermarket, the bottle whose label had been instrumental in her choice of holiday location. Frantically she strove to remember its name and as memory clicked, she blurted, 'A glass of Mateus Rosé, please.'

Immediately Dona Amelia stiffened she sensed she had made an unhappy choice.

'Mateus is a table wine, *senhorita*,' she pounced, 'surely you must be aware of that?'

To Jade's unutterable relief, Jacinta was quick to scoff. 'Oh, Mae, you are so behind the times! Everyone knows that table wines have recently come into fashion as an aperitif, an end-of-the-day or any-time drink, and besides that, young members of English society will not allow themselves to be in-fluenced by tradition, they pride themselves upon an individualism that at times has given rise to some quite outrageous consequences—is that not so, Jade?'

Keeping her mind firmly fixed upon Di who, though young, and English, could not quite be classed as a member of high society, Jade crossed her fingers against any harmful effects that might accrue from deliberately distorting the truth and replied as casually as she was able.

'Indeed, yes, I can think of one friend in particu-lar who delights in flying in the teeth of conven-tion. I have no doubt, Dona Amelia, that you would find some of her actions, and most of her views, quite shocking.'

'English parents are far too lax in their attitudes towards their children,' Dona Amelia sniffed. 'In my opinion, girls such as yourself are given far too much freedom and far too much money with which to indulge their whims. If I were your mother I should not rest while you were roaming a strange country alone. And what of your father, surely he must object?'

'I have no parents,' Jade told her quietly. 'I never knew my father, and Mother died six years ago.'

'I'm sorry, child,' Dona Amelia looked flustered, 'I had no idea that you were an orphan. Still,' she brightened, 'you were obviously left well provided for, which must help to compensate.'

It was at that moment that Jade ought to have corrected the wrongful impression Dona Amelia had obviously formed. She hesitated, a confession trembling on her lips, but allowed herself to be seduced by an insidious inner voice that was insisting: *How lovely to be considered one of the Beautiful People even for a short while! To become part of the impossible dreams you used to dream whenever you read a gossip column or flicked through the pages of a glossy magazine. Such harmless deception can hurt no one so long as you keep the secret to yourself!*

He who hesitates is lost was an adage that had had no particular meaning to her until the moment Diego returned with her drink and words of truth became obliterated by the smile his quizzical look coaxed to her lips. He was the most attractive man she had ever met—was ever likely to meet—a suitable prince for any Cinderella. There and then she decided, not without an inner quiver, that she *would* go to the ball and so store up a fund of memories to sustain her after the clock struck midnight!

Dona Amelia's calculating assessment continued all during dinner, causing Jade to bless the fact that her expensive schooling, cut so dramatically short, had contained lessons in social behaviour during which she had been taught such frivolous things as how to eat artichokes and asparagus unselfconsciously, how to dip daintily into fingerbowls with rose petals floating on their surface, and how never to comment on a meal before it was finished.

Diego had pondered seriously over each course before deciding which dishes would be most suitable for Jade's English palate. 'I hope,' he grinned, 'that you are not one of those girls who needs to starve in order to retain a perfect figure?'

His tone was casual, but the glance that accompanied it was anything but.

Pink-cheeked, feeling that the skin where his eyes had probed was scorching the petals around his rose, she stammered, 'No, in that respect I'm fortunate, I can eat anything I fancy.'

'Good!' He turned teasing eyes upon his sister. 'I get so bored sharing a table with the likes of Jacinta who nibbles like a rabbit and runs to draw a measure around her hips if ever she falls into the temptation of gratifying her sweet tooth.'

'I do not!' Jacinta's laughing response betrayed very real affection for the brother whose anger had so recently held her in awe. 'We cannot all be blessed with bodies lean as a whip and the constitution of a camel that, should circumstances warrant it, can carry on for days without any sort of sustenance. My brother is a nomad at heart,' she assured Jade, 'often he hops across the sea by plane to visit his Arab friends, then disappears for weeks into the desert, yet he remains aggravatingly noncommittal about his activities.'

'What is there to say about the desert?' their

mother intervened, 'except that it is arid, dusty and deserted. And as for the Arabs themselves, there is little about their culture that is appealing. Why you, Diego, should go out of your way to cultivate such people defeats me utterly.'

He frowned, but remained silent while a waiter served *hors d'œuvres*, portions of *chouriço*, wafer-thin slices of ham which, Diego informed Jade, was expertly cured in the cold sunny mountain air of the Sierra Marena and was a noted Portuguese delicacy.

Unhurriedly, he picked up his fork before rebuking his mother mildly: 'You are being unfair, you know as well as I do that even centuries ago the Moors were a sophisticated and cultured people who bestowed many benefits upon our country. Experts at irrigation, they taught us how to grow rice, introduced us to figs and citrus fruits, peaches, bananas and many of their favourite spices. We also have them to thank for the huge groves of almond trees which they originally planted.'

'Yes, Mae,' Jacinta intruded impishly, 'and you cannot deny that you are almost addicted to little cakes made of almonds and honey, as well as to the sweet nougats which also form part of our legacy from the East.'

Dona Amelia's pallid complexion went slightly pink as she interpreted her daughter's teasing words as an accusation of gluttony. She bridled, then stiffly maintained, 'My preference is for good Portuguese food which is simple, sober and conservative, its flavours undisguised by sauces and relying for taste upon the simple excellence of natural produce. Nothing can help to increase the appetite more than the sight of vibrant red and green peppers, saffron-yellow rice, the pink flesh of fish and the white of succulent poultry. We have a saying in this country, *senhorita*,' her dark eyes stabbed Jade's innocent features, '*Half of the joy of eating is in the eyes; half of a woman's worth is in her face.*'

Which doesn't say much for the rest of me! Jade thought ruefully, recognising Dona Amelia's words as a personal attack. For some reason the woman disliked her. Could it be that her possessiveness forced her to regard any girl as a prospective wedge between herself and her adored son? If so, she sighed inwardly, what a pity her fears could not be allayed—and they very soon would be if she were to discover that the girl she seemed to regard as a rival for her son's affections was utterly lacking in both money and social standing!

Dinner, that had begun at ten-thirty, was traditionally a long-drawn-out meal, protracted by lengthy intervals between courses and by leisurely conversation that seemed set to continue far into the night. Around midnight, however, Jade's eyelids began to weigh heavy. It seemed days since she had made her farewells to Di and Gordon before setting out for the airport, yet incredibly it had been mere hours ago, the beginning of the most excitingly eventful day of her entire life. But not even politeness could prevent a yawn escaping from behind a shielding palm, a hint of fatigue that the lynx-eyed Dom Diego saw and immediately acted upon.

Stubbing out the half-smoked cheroot he had been enjoying with his coffee, he rose to place his hands on the back of her chair.

'You have had a long, tiring day, *cara*, please allow me to escort you to your room.'

Dona Amelia and Jacinta waved away her apology, but made no attempt to follow her example when, taking advantage of Diego's proffered arm, she stumbled out of the overcrowded, overheated dining-room.

'Do Portuguese always keep such late hours?' she murmured when finally they stopped outside the door of her room.

'When night falls we are apt to become more alive,' he admitted with a smile, sliding a supporting arm around her waist and drawing her forward until her head was resting upon his chest, nestling close as an infant in search of protection.

All evening she had longed for this moment, aware that dinner had been merely a prelude to a more intimate relationship, yet, eager though she was for the exciting experience to begin, timidity made her tremble.

Softly, reassuringly, Diego spoke above her head. 'No, *cara*, I do not intend to kiss you. Much as I long to, much as I sense your own longing, I refuse to allow our curtain to rise on a cheerless corridor and a girl who is almost asleep in my arms. Tomorrow will be different,' his promise feathered against her ear, 'tomorrow, and the next day, and the day after that ... Time has no meaning for us. We were ordained to meet, ordained to love—aeons ago, lovely snow princess, at the beginning of life itself, you were woven into the pattern of my destiny!'

CHAPTER FOUR

DURING the following days Jade was caught up in a whirlwind of dinners, dances and high society parties. With Diego never far from her side, she became used to drinking cocktails, to chatting with interesting, intelligent people, hobnobbing with the Portuguese aristocracy, eating in exclusive restaurants, and eventually, because of his open display of interest, to being introduced as 'Diego's *namorada*, a young socialite visiting us from England.'

Blessed by her mother's early guidance on points of fashion, make-up and etiquette, she played her part perfectly, mastering her initial nervousness by remembering tips like 'look relaxed'; keep calm'; 'let a smile do the work of an hour's conversation'.

The rich and famous, she was quick to realise, found it a refreshing change to be able to talk to a companion who was friendly, absorbed, and interested; consequently she found the lions of Lisbon deliberately seeking her out, making a beeline towards her immediately she appeared in order to involve her in conversations ranging from politics to sailing, from the latest fashions to her opinion of disco dancing. The most important thing she learnt was always to be herself in exalted company that would not have been in the least impressed had she tried to pretend importance.

Diego, however, took less than kindly to her

amazing conquest of society. When after a particularly hectic party during which she had danced with a succession of partners, sipped like an experimental child glasses of exquisite chilled wine, and enjoyed a delicious supper he escorted her back to the hotel in the early hours of the morning he delayed her sleepy departure into her room with the disgruntled comment.

'All evening you have seemed barely aware of my existence.' Roughly he pulled her into his arms and damned long-standing friends. 'I resent the intrusion of strangers into our lives with their invitations to attend *this* outing, *that* function! Also, I am tired of idle chatter and hot, stuffy rooms. Tomorrow—*today*,' he corrected, 'I want you all to myself, just the two of us together, so that I can take you to all my favourite places.'

Jade thrilled to the thought. She wanted to tell him that she, too, had resented the pressure of people keeping them apart, that even though she had danced and laughed and talked each night away, she had remained constantly alert for a glimpse of his dark head above the crowd, strained to detect his voice amongst the surrounding babble, and that her exhilarated exterior had hidden a tense expectancy as she had waited, hoped, prayed to feel the pressure of his hand upon her elbow. She longed to fling her arms around his neck and pour out everything that she was feeling, but she was still too shy of him, too uncertain of the man whose attitude was possessive, whose intimate asides could jolt her heart from its resting place, but who, as yet, had made not the slightest attempt to kiss her . . .

With his arms strongly enfolding, his breath warm against her cheek, she found it hard to appear calm as she enquired:

'But what about your mother and Jacinta, they may want——'

Forceful fingers sealed her lips to silence the diffident protest. She had been about to suggest that his family might have need of him because neither his mother nor Jacinta seemed to be able to set foot outside the hotel without calling upon him as an escort, but he jumped to a hasty and wrong conclusion.

'For once, you must allow *my* needs to take precedence!' he said imperiously. 'Any previous plans must be cancelled—I refuse to spend one more day dancing like a puppet on the fringe of your attention.' She was shocked by the suddenness with which he released her, then stepped away, his features set hard, his fingers flexing then tightening into knotted fists as if he felt frustration a raging lion within him. That the leash was strained tight was evident when he whipped: 'I will call for you at ten. Be ready, for I do not relish being kept waiting.'

She was too tired to lie awake pondering on his puzzling attitude, but thoughts of him occupied her subconscious to such an extent that promptly at nine o'clock that morning an alarm bell rang in her mind, rousing her to instant wakefulness. She jumped out of bed, had a quick shower, then when a maid arrived with her breakfast managed to snatch quick bites of buttered roll and to sip a cup of coffee while she rummaged in her wardrobe trying to decide which outfit she should wear.

Her range of choice was far from extensive, yet because she had opted for mix-and-match basics she had contrived, with the aid of clever accessories, to achieve such versatility that Jacinta had been prompted to chastise her brother.

'You were so reluctant to bring me on this shopping trip to Lisbon, but now, with Jade as an example, you must see how right I was to insist that my wardrobe was not only inadequate but outmoded. Jade has worn three different outfits each day, yet still she continues to shame me by appearing in yet another chic, sophisticated ensemble.'

If only Jacinta could see the large expanse of wardrobe left empty, Jade mused, sliding hangers along the rail in search of inspiration. Her hand hesitated, hovered, then withdrew from the wardrobe a suit of fine bouclé the colour of bitter chocolate, with a slim skirt and simply-tailored jacket cuffed and collared in a deeper shade of velvet. Thoughtfully she eyed it, then concluded that it offered the ideal solution to the problem of what to wear on an occasion when she had no idea where she would be going nor what other people might be wearing. Because Diego had intimated that they might start their day with a tour of the city, she teamed a cool white tee-shirt with the suit to begin with, then into a roomy handbag she tucked a cashmere sweater and, in case the day should extend into evening, a carefully-folded, embroidered shirt, a gold strand necklace and a tiny spray of expensive scent. She was just putting the finishing touches to her hair when the telephone rang and the hotel receptionist informed her:

'Dom Diego da Luz Pereira da Silves sends his

compliments, *senhorita*, and asks if you would please join him in the foyer as soon as you are able.'

With shaking hands she banged down the telephone receiver, picked up her bag, then without even a last glance into the mirror hastened to meet him, her steps outpaced by racing pulses.

He was waiting with his back to the staircase as she descended, but showing acute perception of her presence he turned with a smile of welcome as she approached the bottom stair. As was usual whenever they met, they were drawn like metal to a magnet. Their hands clasped, their eyes locked to exchange secret, exciting messages.

'I haven't slept for thinking of this moment,' he admitted simply. 'But you, heartless Snow Princess, have obviously been blessed by hours of beautifying sleep and woke, with the bloom of roses upon your cheeks, sparkles of dew in your eyes, the sheen of pale morning sunlight on your hair.'

'Diego,' she whispered, her heart in her eyes, 'you say such beautiful things ...'

'Don't look at me like that,' he urged grimly, 'or I'll be forced to kiss you right here in the foyer.' Less than gently he grabbed her elbow and began propelling her towards the exit. 'Let's get out of here, quick! Already I feel speculative eyes drifting in our direction and I warn you, *cara*, that I intend to be uncompromisingly rude to anyone attempting to delay the onset of what promises to be a glorious day!'

They ran out into the sunshine laughing like children playing truant from school, into the city built upon hills, with steep, broad avenues lined with nightclubs, cinemas, shops, restaurants and

theatres and many gay yellow trams looking old
and overloaded as they bounced upwards towards
the castle crowning all of Lisbon's glory, then
rattled back downwards towards a grassy bank hug-
ging the River Tagus, blue and dancing as a lover's
eyes.

'May we ride on a tram?' Jade burst impulsively
when he began guiding her towards a long, sleek
car.

'A tram ...?' He sounded as if the thought of
riding a tram was completely new to him. Then he
grinned. 'What an inspired thought! A car is certainly more comfortable, but it does limit the view
and I would not want you to remember Lisbon as a
mere succession of bottom stories, pavements, door-
steps and the pedestals of monuments. But I must
warn you, *cara*, to be prepared to be crushed!'

But she was quite happy being crushed in Diego's
protective arms as he shielded her from the digs of
irritable passengers pushing and shoving their way
either into or out of the tram each time it stopped.
Fewer passengers alighted than the moustachioed
driver allowed to clamber aboard and consequently
they found themselves being pushed farther and
farther along the aisle until Diego's shoulders were
braced against the coachwork and Jade's back was
pressed against his hard, muscled chest.

As the atmosphere became hotter and even more
airless he struggled out of his coat and managed,
a little at a time, to loosen his cuffs and roll the
sleeves of his black shirt above his elbows. Then he
wrenched off his tie and partly unbuttoned his
shirt, baring a strong neck and a glint of gold chain
linked to a medallion positioned over the hollow

of his throat. As the tram jolted along she twisted
around in his arms and, conscious of his laughing
eyes upon her face, tried to decipher the inscrip-
tion engraved around the perimeter of the medallion that had stamped up on its surface a crescent
moon, the same heavenly body she had noticed on
his ring. But the symbols were written in Arabic.

'Man is a moon, his dark side hidden,' he trans-
lated for her benefit, taking full advantage of the
crush by tightening his grip upon her hand-span
waist.

'I'm certain that doesn't apply, in your case,' she
teased, made confident enough to flirt a little. 'Such
a claim might be true of some men, but you are no
desert fox, no turbanned son of Satan—on the contrary, you are a very proper, very considerate Portuguese gentleman.'

The tram plunging into shadows cast by towering walls seemed to offer a feasible explanation for
the sudden clouding of his eyes, but with a faint
stirring of unease she noted how his profile had become even more aquiline, and how his usually
humorous mouth had tightened into a thin, derisive smile.

'Portugal stands with its back to Europe, and its
face to Africa,' he reminded her so morosely she felt
an instant chill of fear.

Jade stared, transfixed by an image in her mind's
eye of a man lean as a whip, tanned as leather,
racing a wild Arab stallion across miles of empty
desert, intoxicated by the freedom of space, revell-
ing in his mastery of a mettlesome mount—a man
ridding himself of the frustrations imposed by an
ultra-civilised society, a man whose hooded eyes,

cruel mouth, and hawk-tight features were just
barely recognisable as Diego's!

With a severe jolt the tram jerked her back to
reality so that her wide frightened eyes were
focused once again upon a quizzical mouth and
concerned eyes, deeply blue, deeply tender.

'This tram ride was not such a good idea, *cara*,
you seem quite shocked by the experience. Happily,
the congestion seems to be easing, most of the passengers will be alighting at the next stop, which
will be the terminus. Yes ... seats are becoming
available!'

'In that case, could we stay aboard for the return journey?' she pleaded, her trembling knees
threatening to deprive her of support.

'Certainly, if that is what you wish.' He sounded
amused. 'We will at least be able to enjoy the
comparative comfort of a seat during the descent.'

As a complete contrast to the first part of their
journey the tram was all but empty except for
themselves and a family of peasants who were obviously up for the day to see the sights. They were
dressed rather incongruously, wearing heavily-
embroidered, cumbersome traditional dresses that
must have been handed down throughout the gene-
rations and cherished with a fine disregard of what
was fashionable.

To Jade's amusement, one of their party who had
been entrusted with an ancient camera to record
their historic visit to the capital was persistently
diverted from his object by the exhortations of his
companions to photograph foreign tourists who
must have appeared in their eyes like creatures from
another world, wearing extremes of fashion which,
in their own way, were as outlandish as their own.

Women tourists whose hair was shorter than that of their male companions presented a topsy-turvy aspect that sent them into gales of laughter, followed by a chorus of disapproving, *'Pois, pois'*, which Jade had no trouble interpreting as the equivalent of: ' Whatever will they think of next ...!'

'They look so happy,' she gurgled, forgetting her earlier unease of the man sitting by her side.

'Riches are not a necessary component of happiness,' Diego rebuked without sting. 'These people find fulfilment by living and working with the soil. Illiteracy is still a great problem and luxury to them is a meaningless word, but they are content with an occasional day out and a plentiful supply of indifferent wine. If only city dwellers were to forsake their sybaritic tastes and live as simply as peasants I have no doubt they would be a whole lot healthier and certainly a great deal more contented.'

Jade suppressed an impulse to contradict, to demand fiercely what he knew of poverty, of backbreaking, soul-destroying hours of monotonous labour that drained physical strength to the dregs and left one incapable of doing no more than dragging a weary body home in order to recuperate sufficient energy to cope with the following identical day. But just in time she managed to bite back the indictment, reminding herself that she must not allow the past to intrude into this short, enchanted interlude, that the factory was behind her and that even when her holiday was finished she had decided that nothing would induce her to undertake similar unsuitable employment.

As lightly as she was able, she countered; 'You

surprise me, Diego. I wouldn't have expected to hear a dedicated man-about-town expounding such a theory.'

'Nor would I expect a social butterfly to sympathise with such an idea,' he smiled, lifting her hand to his lips to carefully and precisely kiss each pink fingertip in a way that never failed to arouse rampant responses. 'You, *Princesa de Neze*, were raised a pampered, cherished child, yet surprisingly you are blessed with the virtues of charitableness and selflessness that are usually accredited to the very poor. A consequent effect of the illogicality is that one yearns to continue the cycle by bestowing costly gifts to reward your sweetness, therefore we will never discover how you would react to adversity.'

'No one buys me costly gifts!' she denied indignantly, wounded by the thought of what he would say should he ever discover that she was not the heiress his mother had decided she was.

'Someone will, sweet princess,' he mocked gently, exercising a charm she found irresistible, 'and very soon, I promise you!'

When they left the tram he took her to lunch in a restaurant famous for its *frango churresco*— charcoal-grilled chicken basted with hot pepper sauce, and a dessert of luscious green figs that was too delicious for Jade to resist, even though Diego laughed at her constant efforts to prevent sticky juice from streaming down her chin.

'When the air is filled with the heavy, sweet scent of the fig trees, there is a smell so seductive that the peasants swear it is capable of soothing even an angry bull.'

'Then I must keep some by me,' she quipped, 'in

case I should ever make you angry.'

Lazily he eyed her face, aglow with happy innocence: 'I doubt if you could ever do that, *Princesa de Neze.*'

'Why do you keep calling me that?' she burst out. 'I don't feel the least bit icy and aloof, as that name implies—I'm all warm and cosy and eager for friendship!'

'*Just* for friendship ...?' he quirked, raising one crooked eyebrow.

Friendship was all she dared aspire to! All her timid uncertainty flooded back, causing her face to pinch as the smile faded slowly from her lips.

'There, you see ...!' he frowned. 'Every once in a while some thought seems to frighten you and for a time you become withdrawn as if lonely, yearning for the comfort of familiar sights and faces just as your namesake did, *Princesa de Neze*, the Norwegian princess who married a king of the Algarve. In that sun-baked land her heart pined for the snow peaks of her own country, all winter she seemed to be fading away, so finally the king, because of his great love for her, was forced to allow her to return home. But one morning in spring she looked out of the castle window and cried out for joy, for all the hills were white as if with snow. "No, my dearest," her husband explained, "those are the almond trees that have burst into bloom", and the almond blossom of the Algarve so consoled her that she was able to remain there happily for the rest of her life.

'Do you suppose,' he dropped casually into the conversation as he concentrated upon the green iced wine he was twirling around in his glass, 'that a devoted husband could sufficiently compensate for the loss of one's home and all of one's friends?'

'I ... I ...' Jade's throat was so tight she could barely speak. Was he simply trying to establish a fact, or did he mean ...? Oh, *no*! she gulped; he couldn't *possibly* be asking her ...

'Let's get out of here!' With an impatient jerk he pushed back his chair and almost hauled her out of her seat, giving her barely time to snatch her handbag before ushering her out of the restaurant.

Holding her tightly by the hand, he walked briskly, so deep in thought he seemed oblivious to the fact that she was being forced to run to keep up with him. Her breath was coming in gasps, sweat was trickling between her shoulderblades, when finally they reached the riverside and she was released to flop down panting on the grassy bank.

She had only just managed to master her erratic breathing when he dropped down beside her and shocked her breathless once again with a terse demand.

'Well, Jade, how much longer must I wait for my answer? Tell me, *querida*, are you struggling to find words to reject my proposal or,' his arrogance developed a crack, 'have you made up your mind to marry me?'

CHAPTER FIVE

JADE stared into a mirror, then took a deep breath before tightening shaking fingers around her lipstick and attempting to outline the curve of her trembling bottom lip. She felt physically and mentally exhausted, thrashed by the persistent arguments Diego had expounded in his determination to get her to change her mind.

All afternoon they had walked, supposedly on a sightseeing tour of the city, but the bustling squares, the palace, the cathedral, the shops and the gardens had all merged into a blurred sort of mirage before eyes too dazed to focus. Ruthlessly he had employed every weapon at his command, exploiting the least sign of weakening with a heavy bombardment of flattery, coaxing, and irresistible charm. And yet, although she hadn't the faintest notion how, she had managed to retain sufficient sanity to keep on repeating her first shaken refusal.

'I'm sorry, Diego, but I can't possibly marry you ...'

'Why?' he had demanded, scouring her face with glittering blue ferocity. 'Please don't attempt to trot out the silly argument that we hardly know one another, because you must believe as I do that our encounter at the airport was not a first meeting but more of a reunion of two souls parted during some previous existence! How else can one account for immediate recognition, for instant attraction, for the urge of supposed strangers to kiss and embrace in the manner of lovers?'

Jade had been unbearably moved and not a little shaken when sombrely he had betrayed a fatalism inherited from his Moorish ancestors by declaring: 'We hold no secrets from one another, you and I, for already we have loved, have been as one. Sometimes in my dreams I am tantalised by an almost recaptured ecstasy, I feel the silken quiver of your body against mine, hear your small gasps of pleasure, taste the salt of innocent tears upon my lips, yet always, just as my dream is about to reach fulfilment, you fade out of my arms and I awake savagely frustrated to toss and turn the remainder of the night away. This torment cannot go on!' he had suddenly blazed. 'Marriage would be a mere formality, already I feel you belong to me!'

Reduced to tears by words of truth she found impossible to deny, she had begged him to take her back to the hotel, but adamantly he had refused.

'No, Jade, I will not allow you to run away, to escape amongst the crowd of strangers who descend to separate us at every given opportunity. I'm keeping you by my side for as long as is necessary to discover the reason behind your refusal to accept the inevitable.'

'Is the *senhorita* not well?' The softly-spoken enquiry startled her. She spun round and saw a cloakroom attendant hovering, her expression a mixture of apology and concern. 'I am sorry if I intrude, but your face looks so white and you have sat silently staring for so long ...'

'Oh, I'm fine, thanks.' Jade made an enormous

effort to pull herself together. 'I've had rather a tiring day—sightseeing, you know—so I slipped in here to freshen up, to change my blouse and repair my make-up before rejoining my friend who is ordering dinner for us both.'

The woman's face brightened. 'These men!' she exclaimed, throwing up her hands in a gesture of despair. 'When will they realise that we women possess only half their share of stamina? I would urge you to rest longer, *senhorita*, but as it is, you have left yourself barely enough time to enjoy your meal before the *fadista* is due to begin.'

'*Fadista* ...?' Jade queried.

'*Sim*,' she nodded. 'This restaurant is noted for its *fado* singers. The *fado* is regarded by some as a national tradition, but it really belongs mainly to Lisbon. I am certain that you will enjoy the singing very much, *senhorita*, but you must not make the mistake of talking once the music begins or you will become very unpopular, because the *fado* is always taken seriously by the audience as well as by the performers.'

Diego was waiting for her outside the entrance to the dining-room and immediately she spotted him she realised that he was champing at the bit.

'Where on earth have you been?' he clamped. Then, pulling rein on his temper, he apologised, 'I'm sorry, but you have been absent for so long I had begun to suspect that you had deserted me. However,' he tucked her hand into the crook of his elbow and smiled his approval, 'the result is well worth waiting for—you look *bonita, minha amor*.'

The restaurant was crowded, but they were led, as if it had been specially reserved for them, to-

wards a table set in a secluded alcove that allowed
them privacy yet provided a commanding view of a
circular patch of floor space which was crowded
with couples dancing. All main lights had been
switched off to allow the full effect of lighted
candles set into coloured glass globes that were casting a soft, intimate glow across each table. Somewhere out of sight a band was playing music attuned to an atmosphere that was luxurious almost
to the point of seduction; deferential waiters serv-
ing richly aromatic dishes from silver salvers; vel-
vet-covered seats; exquisite flower arrangements,
spotless table linen, and a clientele wearing costly
but informal dress—a factor that had evidently in-
fluenced Diego's choice of venue.

'This restaurant has become a favourite of business men wishing to entertain overseas clients newly
arived in Lisbon,' he explained, seemingly able to
read her mind. 'Both the food and the entertainment provided are typically Portuguese and the
atmosphere is conducive to either business talk or
purely to enjoyment. Which is why I chose it,' his
voice suddenly crisped. 'First of all we talk—then
later ...!'

His meaningful pause, the stress he placed upon
his final word caused a welter of confusion to erupt
inside her. There must be no later! Somehow she
had to convince him that for them there could be
no future together, that once her holiday was finished their paths would diverge in completely opposite directions. But the moment for truth had
passed; she could not offend his dignity by telling
him that he had proposed marriage to a girl whose
status was equal to that of a peasant, one who,

after two weeks of indulgence, would be left with just enough money to supply the requisite tips.

He waited until the wine waiter had served the champagne he had ordered, then when the bottle had been replaced in its bed of cracked ice, he lifted his glass and with humour playing around his mouth he toasted: 'To a dream—may it soon become reality!'

As he lifted his glass to drain it to the dregs candlelight flickered across his half-closed lids revealing eyes ablaze with inner laughter. Hurt stabbed Jade like a dagger, cutting her confidence to shreds as doubts that had always lurked near the surface of her mind rose up in force to strengthen her suspicion that he was amused by her naïveté, entertained by the confused, awkward shyness that kept her tongue-tied and rendered her incapable of meeting his eyes. Fool that she was for taking him seriously! How could she ever have imagined that this man, this mixture of devil and saint, nomad and *fidalgo* could have contemplated for even one moment taking a nonentity such as herself as his wife? The arrogant *fidalgo*, bored by his enforced attendance upon his family, had been in search of diversion and had found for himself a simple, amusing plaything!

Pride reared its head, tinging her voice with the coolness of the wine frosting against the rim of her glass. 'It has been said,' she tilted shakily, 'that one may judge a man's character by the way in which he treats those less fortunate than himself. In the old days the aristocracy employed jesters to titillate their humour and clowns to lighten their boredom—it seems to me, *senhor*, that having filled

the same purpose it is I who should be wearing a
cap and bells!'

She would have jumped up from the table and
run, but for the fact that her eyes were blinded by
tears which, mercifully, when she blinked them
away became sizzled into extinction on fiery cheeks.

'Of what are you accusing me, Jade?'

Her sensitive soul reacted with a lurch to the
level of hurt in the question quietly projected across
the width of the table. She almost cried out with
the hurt inflicted by his duplicity, but managed to
school her agony so that it could be hidden behind
a mask of offended pride.

'I'm charging you with cruel deceitfulness,' she
choked, 'and heartless pretence. I suppose,' she
accused shakily, 'I must have appeared fair game
to a man such as yourself, a timid mouse only too
eager to be fooled into believing the fairy tales you
wove around our so-called romance, eager to lap up
your flattery, to believe every honeyed lie. I imagined you to be a gentleman, *senhor*, a man of
honour ...' She had to fight back tears before she
could go on. 'Although I must admit that you are
clever and experienced enough to have made certain that no concrete charge can be laid against
you—you seduced only with words, with looks,
with the occasional light caress. I feel ravished,' her
voice faded to a low whisper as her green eyes,
wounded with disbelief, accused her tormentor,
'yet in reality you haven't so much as kissed me ...'

Because the lighting was kind, they must have
appeared to any casual observer to be a man and a
woman happy in each other's company, engaged in
normal conversation, but not even the shadows

lurking beyond the glowing candlelight could soften the harshness that had appeared on Diego's features, or cloud the blazing blue fury in his eyes.

Jade quivered from his lance of displeasure and sat with eyes downcast, her hands tightly clenched in her lap, looking in her silk, primly-collared shirt with full, tight-wristed sleeves, like a sad, solemn choirboy.

'If I were the despicable sort of rake you have just implied, would I have asked you to marry me?'

His cold wave of words drenched over her, leaving her gasping. He was two separate entities—one that she knew, the other merely guessed at. The courteous, softly-spoken Dom Diego had fled, leaving in his place a stern-faced, hawk-eyed stranger with a jawline haughtily outthrust and eyes rampant with the pride of Adam himself. Jade felt cowed as a slavegirl who had earned the displeasure of her master, yet from somewhere she dredged up enough spirit to state her honest opinion.

'If I had been rendered sufficiently gullible, if insight hadn't torn the blinkers from my eyes, your proposal might have provided sufficient inducement to encourage me to share your bed!'

She was never to know what reply he might have given. All she heard was his sharply-indrawn breath before noise exploded all around them—the enthusiastic applause of an audience welcoming the appearance of a woman in black who was spotlighted in the centre of a darkened, empty dance floor bowing and waving to her fans. As her accompanying guitarists began to play, Jade felt grateful for the heavy background silence that precluded so much as a whisper from Diego, whose oppressive shadow was emanating violence.

For almost an hour the woman sang words meaningless to Jade, but the nostalgic, mournful melodies became forever associated in her mind with despair and almost unbearable heartbreak. Conscious that her hands were tightly clenched, her body taut, she willed herself to relax as the music washed over her, beginning like a slowly-murmuring stream, then suddenly descending; racing like a whirlpool, then simmering to a stillness covering deep, hidden depths. It was the music of Portugal, a vocal portrait of its people, Jade mused, her mind upon Jacinta who seemed at one moment a fatalist and in the next a rebel; apathetic, then suddenly bursting with energy. Then here was her brother who at first had seemed kind but who she now knew could be harsh and arrogant; who could be gentle, mystical, poetical, then could confound with a display of sarcasm and a streak of cruelty doubtless inherited from Moorish ancestors who had thought nothing of draining their women of the last drop of pleasure, then shamelessly handing them over for auction to the highest bidder.

Good manners kept them chained to their seats during the lengthy recital, but even as the singer was taking her first bow Diego showed his impatience to leave by jumping to his feet to begin ushering Jade out of the restaurant. The audience were settling down to enjoy the singer's first encore, yet he seemed impervious to astonished looks as, with a determined hand upon Jade's elbow, he guided her through a maze of tables.

Outside, the air was balmy, the night-shrouded

city alive with twinkling lights, bustling with people in search of enjoyment. But she knew that there was no enjoyment in store for her, just a battle with the elements of anger written across Diego's set features. The proud *fidalgo* was outraged. Doubtless he was unused to plain speaking, to having his motives questioned and his overtures rebuffed. Being a master of pretence, he would no doubt try to protest that he had been misunderstood, she told herself as she was hurried along, forced to keep up with his pace, but she would refuse to listen, would fight off every advance from behind her newly-regained armour of common sense.

Her courage faltered when, without a word of explanation, he swung her in the direction of an entrance into a public garden. Once they had become swallowed up inside a shroud of darkness he jerked her to a halt and spun her round to face him. She drew in a long, deep breath, preparing to marshal her arguments, only to be completely deflated by arms that pulled her roughly forward into a crushing embrace and by a hard, angry mouth that swooped to silence the questions trembling on her lips.

The suddenness of the assault was shocking, yet it was in no way as devastating as the emotions aroused when she felt the touch of a man's plundering mouth against her own for the very first time. If Diego had been aware of the extent of her innocence perhaps, even in anger, he would have been a little more tender, but as it was he was merciless, wielding his skill in seduction like a whip, thrashing her emotions bare, punishing her with passion until she collapsed against him, a sobbing, quivering prisoner.

'Now do you understand why I did not kiss you— why I never *dared* to kiss you,' he charged hoarsely, burying his face against her silken hair. 'I had to force myself to wait, because I knew, *namorada*, that once we had kissed I would never be able to let you go. You were right in one respect, Jade— I do pretend ...' She quivered as his mouth began tracing the gentle, pulsating curve of her neck. 'I pretend to be civilised, but at heart I'm a savage, and just like a savage I'll fight with no holds barred to retain possession of what is mine! I have tried to convince you of my love, I was even prepared to wait until your timidity had been overcome, but,' his fingers gripped deeply into her waist, 'you tried me too far when you accused me of deceit—a failing that is abhorrent to me. Put an end to this nightmare, I beg of you, Jade, promise that you will marry me *immediately*!'

But the terse, almost angry plea made little impression on her confused, storm-racked mind. If she had been thrown unexpectedly into a whirlpool she could not have been more disorientated, felt more battered, more desperately in need of a lifeline with which to haul herself back to the shore of sensible normality.

He could not be serious! Although his lips had been urgent, roughened by desire, his caresses intimate to the point of possessiveness, they had to be part of a ploy, the weapons of a charmer with seduction on his mind, The sort of man Di had obviously had in mind when as they said their goodbyes she had waved an admonishing finger and warned,

'Mind you're not swept off your feet by one of those macho Mediterranean guys we've heard so much about, who enjoy torrid fortnightly affairs right throughout the tourist season! English girls are especially attractive to them because of their fair complexions and supposedly lax morals; from all accounts, they can be passionate, subtle, and deceivingly considerate until they get what they want—but afterwards they're quick to say *"Adeus, senhorita*, see you again next year, *perhaps*!"'

But Diego was not like that! Even to think of him in such a context was an insult to the proud *fidalgo* who placed honour above all things, whose sincerity was such he had even asked her to marry him ...

'*Querida*,' gently he shook her out of her daze, 'I am waiting for your answer.'

When his dark head lowered, threatening a repeat of the turbulence aroused by his first hungry kiss, she jerked a protest. 'No, please don't, Diego. I must talk to you!'

'Why must you?' he groaned. 'We communicate so much better without words.' But he did as she wished and contented himself with rubbing his cheek against her silken swathe of hair, softly murmuring, 'Already you have told me all I need to know, sweet Jade, the moment our lips met I sensed your passion rising to meet mine. The strength of that passion shocked you, little one, did it not? I felt a jolt running through your body, then a trembling that began when you felt you might become devoured. You have no need to fear me, *querida*,' he husked, his tender, searching lips against her temple driving her sensitive nerves demented. 'I can be savage with those who merit savagery; merciless to the cruel and untamed, but with an orphaned fawn I would always be gentle, tender, and full of compassion.'

Tossed like a straw on an urgent current, she pressed her cheek closer to his chest to draw strength from his powerfully thudding heartbeat.

'You make me sound like an abandoned waif,' she protested weakly.

'Aren't you, orphan child?' he teased lightly, but with an undercurrent of solemnity. 'Sometimes you have a lost look that never fails to tighten my heartstrings, the look of a lonely soul aching to love and be loved. Money and position are not enough, are they, *cara*?' he urged softly. 'I want to fill the void in your heart—why won't you let me?'

He must have felt her sudden stiffening, but he made no comment; instead he enfolded her closer and waited, sensing her search for difficult words.

Jade found it almost impossible to think with the thudding of his heart in her ears and the warmth of his body wrapping her within a cocoon of euphoria, a trance-like state in which she could almost, but not quite, persuade herself that no harm could come from unconditional surrender, that she should not endanger the prospect of a gloriously happy future by trying clumsily to explain what, after all, had been a very minor deception. At the end of the battle, however, conscience emerged the victor.

'Diego,' she gulped.

'Yes, beloved?' He remained very still, tensed as if to combat shock.

'I ... I'm not as rich as your mother seems to think.'

'*Por amor de Deus!* Is that all?' He exploded into laughter so humourless that she sensed he was battling between amusement and anger.

'Also,' she stumbled on, eager to confess all, 'I possess no social status.'

Her confession was strangled into extinction by an angry kiss that stamped his impatience, scorn, and enormous relief upon her trembling mouth. 'Your status is unimpeachable, inasmuch as you are as immaculate as the day you were born,' he chastised hoarsely. 'How dare you torment me with such trivia, how could you even suspect that I would allow such petty details to influence my decision to make you my wife, to take you home with me to the Castelo de Seteais as my beautiful bride! I had imagined that at the very least I had a rival, someone to whom you were already promised!' He glared savage relief into her bemused eyes. 'For that you deserve to be punished,' he scolded, then suddenly jerked her hard against his heart, 'but I will forgive you,' he promised thickly, 'on condition that you repeat after me: "*Yes, Diego, I love you! Please, Diego, let me become your bride.*"'

CHAPTER SIX

'EVERY girl is expected to look beautiful on her wedding day,' Jacinta sighed ecstatically, 'but you are exceptionally so, Jade! Indeed, for the past two weeks you have put every woman in Lisbon in the shade! There is a luminosity about you,' she paused, searching for words, 'it is as if my brother has lighted a beacon of love inside you that is sending out beams of happiness. Do you love him so very much ...?' she questioned wistfully.

Jade stepped away from a mirror and carefully draped her wedding veil over her bed. 'Of course I do,' she replied, a soft blush rising in her cheeks. 'I need hardly point out to you how very lovable he is.'

'Sometimes he can be,' Jacinta admitted thoughtfully. 'But then again, there are occasions when lovable would be the very last word one would use to describe him.'

Jade's lips twitched. Jacinta's wishes never seemed to run parallel to her brother's will and as a consequence there were many minor altercations during which she always seemed to come off worst. 'Unfortunately,' Jade smiled to soften the blow of criticism, 'you do seem to have a tendency to arouse in him a dominating streak, but he always has your interests at heart. He strives, I think, to take the place of a just, not too indulgent father.'

Still smarting from an argument she had lost to

her brother the previous evening, Jacinta snorted, 'Huh! There is as much similarity between my brother and an indulgent father as there is between Arab and Berber!'

Jade was puzzled by the comparison. 'They are both of the same race, are they not?'

'Diego would argue not,' she snapped. 'Although Arab and Berber have intermarried for over a thousand years, tribes of pure Berbers still survive in remote mountain regions and these people, who are my brother's friends, have a high regard for the truth. Their reputation for honesty is as well known as that of the Arabs who, according to the Berbers who look upon them with contempt, are the greatest liars and deceivers on earth. Sometimes,' her indignation boiled over, 'I swear Diego is more Berber than Portuguese. Do you know, last night he threatened to ban me from your wedding simply because he found me out in one small, insignificant lie! Were it not for the fact that I managed to persuade him that you would be upset by my absence I would be confined to my room this very minute!'

Jade turned away to hide a smile. Jacinta was well known for her flights of fancy and the simile she had drawn between the iron-willed Berbers and her ultra-civilised brother was ludicrous. Nevertheless, after a moment's thought, she frowned as doubts began to nag. Had she been explicit enough when she had tried to explain her true circumstances? Should she have tried harder during the past two weeks, during which his mood had been so wonderfully mellow, to ensure that her past could cast no shadow over their future? But then, she consoled herself, he had been so impatient of

wasted time whenever she had attempted to broach
the subject—there had been so much to do, so many
arrangements to be made, that every precious,
snatched moment had been filled with kisses ...

A rap upon the door drew Jacinta's attention and
as she ran to open it Jade tensed, anticipating the
arrival of Dona Amelia, the woman who was casting the only blight upon her happiness. Her heart
sank when Diego's mother bustled into the room
looking as flustered, agitated and displeased as she
had from the moment she had been informed of her
son's impending wedding.

'What, are you not dressed yet?' she scolded at
the sight of Jade, whose progress, because of Jacinta's constant interruptions, had reached only the
stage of donning a silken underslip.

'I'm ready except for my dress and veil,' she
assured her hastily, 'and it won't take a minute to
slip into those.'

'Just as well,' Dona Amelia snapped. 'Already
Diego has left for the church. Oh, the shambles!'
she wailed, throwing her hands in the air. 'It will
be a miracle if everything goes off as it should.
Never have I known such haste—such *unseemly*
haste——' she stressed, eyeing Jade with a look
almost of dislike. 'If you had been prepared to wait
just a few weeks longer the marriage could have
taken place at the Castelo and been attended by all
our friends. But *no*!' she glared. 'My son is so be-
sotted he has to be married the soonest possible day
that can be arranged, despite the fact that it means
the ceremony has to take place in a strange church
in the presence of guests who are no more than
casual acquaintances. I still maintain,' her suspi-

cious eyes challenged Jade, 'that given a few more weeks you could have arranged for someone to travel from England in order to support you on this very important day. You must have *some* relatives, Jade, or, if not, at least one close friend?'

Seeing Jade's look of distress, Jacinta remembered her supportive role of chief bridesmaid and immediately jumped to her rescue.

'Jade cannot dredge relatives out of thin air, not even to please you, Mae, and she has already explained that her best friend, herself just recently married, is too involved with the upheaval of settling into a new home to be able to spare the time to come. She has, I believe, promised to pay you a visit at the first possible opportunity, Jade, has she not?'

Jade nodded, then turned away to hide a quick surge of tears. If only Di were here to help assuage her fears, she thought wistfully, groping for a tissue to mop up moisture from heavily-laden lashes. To listen to Jacinta, one could be forgiven for imagining that Di and Gordon were in the process of moving into a mansion instead of the modest tworoomed flat they had recently rented. She had managed to get in touch with Gordon by telephoning his bank. His first reaction to the news of her impending marriage had been a startled silence followed by cautious congratulations. His response to her invitation to attend had, however, been very definite.

'Nothing would give me more pleasure than to be able to say yes, Jade, but the truth of the matter is that we're flat broke, every spare penny has gone on furnishing the flat—I couldn't even scrape up the fare for Di alone, much less the two of us.'

Di's following letter, which she had received only that morning, had confirmed everything that Gordon had said in an outpouring of words as flamboyantly contradictory as her moods, expressing joy and doubt, enthusiasm and caution within the space of each scrawled sentence.

Neatly, Jade had folded the flimsy pages into a small square and tucked it inside her slip next to her heart, hoping its presence would help her to feel a little less forlorn, less terrifyingly lonely, when she walked down the aisle towards Diego.

'If you are ready, Jade, I'll help you on with your dress.' With cheeks as pink as the frothy tulle dress she had chosen as her wedding outfit, Jacinta approached with a swathe of white satin draped over her arm. Obediently, Jade lowered her head and felt her heart begin a mad tattoo when cool satin caressed her warm skin before sliding down past her waist to settle without a crease or fold a fraction above the ground.

'The length is exactly right, I think,' Jacinta approved with her head cocked to one side, 'but you must remember to lift your skirt whenever necessary, otherwise the hem might become soiled.'

To their consternation, while they were busy fastening a row of tiny satin-covered buttons that began at the neckline and plunged downward beyond the waist, Dona Amelia began to sob.

'Whatever is wrong?' Jacinta admonished, half cross, half amused.

Her mother shook her head so vigorously she seemed in danger of dislodging the elegant plume from her hat. 'It is nothing,' she gasped, 'merely that I am overcome by emotion brought by memories of my own wedding day and your dear, departed father. Fate is so unkind,' she sobbed. 'Because of a mettlesome horse I was robbed of a husband—because Diego decided to fit in a business trip to London while we were here in Lisbon I have been robbed of a son.'

'How can you say such a thing to Jade!' Jacinta rounded furiously.

When she seemed set to continue in the same vein, Jade interrupted quietly. 'Would you leave us for a short while, please, Jacinta, while I talk privately with your mother?'

Her uncharacteristic note of authority took Jacinta so much by surprise that she nodded and left the room without further argument. Dona Amelia was still sobbing noisily into her handkerchief when Jade laid a tentative hand upon her shoulder.

'Please stop crying and listen to me for just a moment, Dona Amelia.' Quaking inwardly, she schooled her voice to calmness as softly she pleaded, 'Much of the unhappiness in the world is caused by things being left unsaid, so I hope you will not think me presumptuous when I tell you that I know exactly how you're feeling. I, too, have known the loneliness of being parted from a loved one, but whereas my loss is final yours need not be if only you could bring yourself to look upon me not as an outsider who has stolen your son, but as a daughter eager to become once again part of a family. If you could do that, Dona Amelia, we could walk not simply side by side, but together.'

When a lengthy silence fell Jade felt certain that

she was about to be rebuffed by the proud woman whose distress had reduced her to tears. But when Dona Amelia finally looked up Jade saw to her relief that her expression had softened, her eyes were full of hope and dawning respect.

'You are very generous,' she cleared her throat, 'yet in your position you don't need to be.'

'Nor do we need to be rivals,' Jade assured her gravely. 'I'm certain that Diego has enough love to spare for both of us.'

For a second longer Dona Amelia studied Jade's earnest face, then, seemingly reassured, she rose to her feet to admit, pathetically shamefaced, 'From the very beginning I have harboured doubts about you. Even in Portugal, such an air of innocence is rare, which is why I found it hard to believe that your unworldliness could be genuine. I believe it now.' She reached out a shaking hand to pat Jade's cheek. 'Now I can be happy for myself as well as for my son.' As if the admission had embarrassed her, she drew herself erect and adopted a brisk tone. 'But you must finish dressing, I have detained you long enough. *Adeus, minha filha*, until we meet in church.'

With the last obstacle to her happiness removed, Jade submitted to Jacinta's ministrations in a state of joyful euphoria. The day now promised to be perfect. In less than an hour she would become Senhora da Silves—a wonderful new heading with which to begin the most glorious chapter of her life!

When Jacinta had arranged her coronet and veil she stepped back with a sigh of satisfaction tinged with awe. From a circlet of orange-blossoms pinned firmly on to a coil of silver-sheened hair fell a veil of tulle, an unblemished white cloud that stirred and billowed at Jade's least movement, then settled around her, a soft frame of purity. As she stared at her reflection in a mirror, Jade felt pleased that she had ignored Jacinta's well-meaning advice and insisted upon stark simplicity, choosing a dress utterly devoid of frills, flounces or embroidery, its impact relying solely upon smooth uncluttered lines and superb satin that captured her youthful slenderness within a heart of shimmering pearl.

Panic assailed her when Jacinta handed her the bouquet Diego had ordered specially in order to convey a secret message to his bride, a mixture of lilies—a tribute to her purity, orange-blossoms. the symbol of virginity, and roses, which implied that he believed her incorruptible, all their stems bound round with strips of palm, the leaf, he had told her with a wicked glint, that was always associated with victory ...

She ought to have been reassured by this message of high esteem, but instead she felt fear, fear of what might happen should she ever slip from her elevated pedestal.

'*Meu Deus!* Your face is as white as marble, Jade! If you are having last-minute doubts then dismiss them,' Jacinta teased, 'and for heaven's sake try to smile, otherwise my brother will think he is about to marry a penitent nun!'

Slowly the bridal car made its way down a sloping road lined with black and white mosaic pavements, past the splendid fountain with six spouts which Diego had sworn were reserved in strict order for: the nobility, for women, for soldiers, for sailors, for servants and for galley slaves; along a façade of imposing buildings between which Jade caught a glimpse every now and again of the thriving fishing port from which *varinas* burdened with cumbersome petticoats hurried, carrying wicker baskets full of wet fish dripping moisture on to the tops of their heads.

When the car turned away from teeming streets and into a quiet space panic burst to life in her throat at the sight of a fairytale tower that might have been built of ivory with, next to it, the honey-coloured walls of a church built on the very spot from which explorers had set sail in search of knowledge and which, it was said, owed its existence to profits accrued from the gems and spices they had brought back from the Orient.

On the arm of an elderly friend of Dona Amelia's who had courteously volunteered his services, Jade entered the south porch and was confronted by a high-domed, wood-panelled interior warmed by the jewelled glow from a magnificent stained glass window. She heard the muted strains of an organ, became vaguely aware that Jacinta was fussing with her train, then, encouraged by her escort, she took her first tentative step forward just as a choir of children's voices burst into a hymn of praise.

The slow dignified walk to reach Diego's side seemed to stretch into infinity, giving her ample time to experience panic, remorse, doubts and worst of all an agonising yearning for the presence of her mother, or even just the sight of some face amongst the crowd of strangers that was smiling for her alone.

Her escort tightened his grasp upon her arm

when he felt a nervous tremor shudder through her slender frame, then with relief he felt tension draining from her as he handed her into the care of her solemn bridegroom, his heart brilliantly displayed in eyes of blazing Tagus blue.

Diego made his responses in a voice firm with authority, but hers were a mere thread of sound that barely penetrated past the first row of crowded pews. Yet when the time came for him to slide the wedding ring on to her finger, the slender, satin-cuffed hand she extended towards him was perfectly steady. She could never afterwards recall the exact moment when their marriage became finalised, but when Diego bent his head to place a tender, moving kiss upon her lips she sensed that she had just received her very first kiss from her husband.

Her heart was soaring, her steps light as gossamer, as with her hand tucked into the crook of his arm Diego escorted her down the aisle while the organ pealed, the choir's voices escalated high as the domed ceiling, and bells began to ring, joyful, silvery cadences holding a message of hope she knew she would retain in her memory for the rest of her life.

They had little time to talk during the short drive back to the hotel where the reception was to be held, no opportunity even to share a kiss as the sleek, beribboned bridal car with its expanse of plate glass windows left them exposed as goldfish in a bowl to the inquisitive eyes of well-wishers who smiled and waved from the thronged pavements lining their route.

Diego kept a tight clasp upon her hand and

fought to erase from his expression all traces of the impatience he was feeling to have his beautiful bride to himself. But his frustration boiled over into words he muttered under his breath as the car drew up in front of the hotel.

'Whoever it was that said that "life is but a long, sweet torment" must have had a moment like this one in mind!'

He caught his breath when Jade turned to send him a sweet, admonishing smile. 'Be patient, dear Diego! Just a few more hours will see the true beginning of the rest of our lives.'

A crowd had gathered outside the hotel to see the arrival of the newlyweds, black-skirted locals with a proprietorial interest in the arrival of one of their aristocracy, jostled elbow to elbow with goggle-eyed tourists anxious to catch a glimpse of the English girl who, it was rumoured, upon her arrival on holiday mere weeks ago had captured the heart of one of Portugal's richest and most eligible bachelors.

A great sigh of delight rose from the throats of the crowd when Jade stepped out of the car giving, in her shimmering dress and billowing veil, a reminder to the more poetical of a priceless pearl set against a backcloth of virginal cloud. Smiling with pleasure, her green eyes sparkling with happiness, she waved acknowledgement to the crowd, then jolted to a halt before the steps of the hotel, transfixed by a glimpse of the familiar amongst the sea of anonymous faces. She had almost convinced herself that she was mistaken, had even forced a leaden step forward, when an excited, high-pitched voice rose above the babble of the crowd to confirm her worst suspicions.

'It *is* Miss High and Mighty, Ted, I told you it was! *Jade!*' A frantic hand waved high in the air. 'It's me—*Kath!*'

Diego must have felt her stiffen, must have sensed that for some reason she had been rendered completely immobilised, because to the delight of the crowd he swept her into his arms and carried her over the threshold of the hotel.

He just had time to set her down on her feet before Jacinta and her mother arrived, followed in quick succession by the remainder of their wedding guests. For almost an hour Jade stood by Diego's side mechanically acknowledging the congratulations and good wishes of guests who filed past them into the huge reception room inside which a buffet luncheon was laid out waiting to be served.

She must have appeared as normal, because her smile that felt frozen on to stiff, cold lips caused no raised eyebrows, no adverse comment, yet she sensed from Diego's puzzled glances that he was aware of and concerned by her distress. Upon the arrival of his mother and sister, he had slipped from her side to exchange a few quick words with the manager of the hotel, and as the last of their guests trickled past them the reason behind his short absence became suddenly and devastatingly clear when Jade saw the manager ushering before him a bemused-looking couple wearing typical tourist apparel that contrasted incongruously against the ultra-smart outfits worn by the cream of Lisbon society.

Diego's words, his pleased smile, turned a knife in her breast, betraying as it did so little knowledge of the threat looming over their happiness. 'As these people are obviously acquaintances of yours,' he murmured before they came within earshot, 'I sent a message, asking them to attend the reception. I am delighted your friends turned up so unexpectedly, and at such an appropriate time.'

Appropriate! Jade thought wildly, digging sharp fingernails into her palms. *Ill-timed, detrimental, catastrophic!* were far more suitable terms! Kath, her former workmate, though not malicious, had earned a reputation of being a pretentious snob. Name-dropping, and veiled insinuations that she moved in higher social circles than most, was her main vanity—that, and a tendency to blurt out tactless remarks.

Jade braced for disaster that descended even quicker than she had expected.

'*Well*, Miss High and Mighty!' Kath ran forward to gush. 'You're certainly living up to your name! The girls will never believe what I have to tell them when I get back to work. Congratulations!' she beamed, then swung calculating eyes upon Diego's slightly stunned expression. 'You always swore to marry money, my dear, and it looks as if you've managed to live up to your promise!'

Somehow Jade hid her tortured feelings behind a composed reply, even managed not to reveal to Kath that her thoughtless words had turned her wedding reception into a wake. Diego had not responded to Kath's remarks with so much as a twitch of a muscle, yet one appalled glance in his direction had confirmed that his eyes were no longer a bright dancing blue, but dark pools of inscrutability.

The last faint hope of survival she had harboured faded when he bowed towards Kath then suavely enquired of her embarrassed, perspiring husband:

'With your permission, *senhor*, I should like to further your wife's acquaintance over a glass of champagne? Perhaps,' his cold eyes flickered over Jade's white face, 'you would favour me by keeping my wife company and entertaining her with reminders of the happy existence she has enjoyed ... up until now.'

CHAPTER SEVEN

DIEGO drove south to the Algarve, taking the most direct route possible to reach his home, the Castelo da Seteais, Castle of the Seven Sighs, where they had arranged to spend their honeymoon.

Jade had changed into a dress of pale grey—the colour of penitence—and with her mane of silver hair tied back with a bright green ribbon for coolness, she looked little older than a child. But as she sat pale and subdued by Diego's side watching first the hotel and then the outskirts of Lisbon, disappearing from view, he spared not so much as a glance for his new bride.

He, too, had changed into a dark open-necked shirt and casual slacks that lent an air of relaxation to his pantherish limbs. But there was nothing relaxed about the profile she was studying out of the corner of her eye—a rigid sweep of jaw terminating in an sternly outthrust chin. She bit her lip and turned away, hoping her misery might be eased by studying a countryside full of strange new sights and sounds; corners full of deep, cool shadows, vacant village streets baking beneath the heat of a noonday sun.

She had imagined that this drive would have been so different, a leisurely tour during which they would drop in on one of the many magical coves Diego had told her were honeycombed with caves and grottoes; that he would eagerly identify for her benefit some of the unfamiliar cork, almond, olive, carob, cypress and eucalyptus trees and even explain the purpose of the soot-black pigs rooting beneath them.

But the hilltop windmills, the rolls of freshly-peeled cork bark, the Moorish fortress and chimneys shaped like miniature lighthouses, were all allowed to pass without comment during their silent journey.

When finally the atmosphere became too oppressive to be borne, Jade summoned up sufficient courage to plead:

'I know you're angry with me, Diego, but please don't judge me too harshly until I've had a chance to explain.'

'Your friend has done all the explaining that is necessary.' The harsh grating of his voice gave startling insight into the depth of his disillusion-ment. 'How you must be cursing fate for revealing you as a cheap, scheming adventuress who set out deliberately in search of a wealthy husband!'

'It wasn't like that at all!' she cried, appalled by his sharp thrust of cruelty.

'No? Are you saying that your friend fabricated all the feminine confidences you had supposedly shared with her and the rest of your workmates? I find that hard to believe, especially when you took such pains to paint a completely different picture of your life. It would not have made the least difference to me had you admitted to a deprived back-ground—indeed, such misfortune could only have added to your appeal; it is the web of lies and deceit you spun that I find unforgivable.'

Once begun, he seemed unable to stem the flow

of savage recrimination. Feeling beaten by many stripes, Jade sat twisting her fingers in her lap, her bright head drooping as she fought back the surge of tears aching behind her eyes.

'Spain, our neighbouring country, is notorious for the attraction it holds for girls such as yourself,' his cold voice continued. 'Why did you choose Portugal as your hunting ground? Is it because Spain has become so saturated with scheming English girls in search of husbands that Spaniards have grown wary? Have the packs of female predators decided to turn their attention upon Portugal because here they expect to find less competition and a probable surfeit of susceptible men?' She jerked up her head to gasp a protest, but was rendered dumb by the cynical twist of his lips that caused a hook to catch in some deep hidden part of her, gouging a wound eternity would not heal. 'If so,' he continued, uncaring of her pain, 'once news of your easy conquest has been circulated we must expect an invasion of mercenary maidens to our shores!'

'Stop it, Diego!' she jerked through clenched teeth. 'Stop torturing yourself, and me, with unfounded suspicion. I had imagined, even though our acquaintance has been so short, that you knew me better than to include me in such calculated conspiracy. It is true that I have no family, no job, no home, but I didn't come to Portugal hoping to remedy those defects, I came merely for a holiday.'

'And from where,' he hissed, sounding threateningly unconvinced, 'did you obtain sufficient money to enable you to book into Lisbon's most expensive hotel and to supply a wardrobe that has moved even my spoiled, clothes-conscious sister to envy?'

'I ... I won some money in a sort of lottery,' she stumbled, wondering why the truth should sound so unconvincing, 'and my friend Di persuaded me to invest it in a holiday.'

Immediately his frown darkened she knew she had used the wrong word—to invest: to speculate with money in the hope of gain! Obviously, the implication had not passed him by.

'I felt so disorganised, so uncertain of whether or not I was doing the right thing,' she blurted desperately, 'that I hadn't even the vaguest notion which country to visit. It was pure chance, a glance at an empty wine bottle, that helped me to decide.'

'*Chance! Speculation!*' His foot plunged down upon the accelerator, sending the car racing along the road at terrific speed. 'It appears to me that your life has been run on the lines of a lottery—*with myself as the prize idiot!*'

As he continued driving at demoniacal speed, rich luscious land flashed past the car window, prim olive groves, one minute softly green, the next whitening like velvet at the stroke of the wind; earth burnt orange by the sun; small farmhouses, and vineyards stretched like a mantle of blue-green silk across the hillsides with, above them, ridge after ridge of moorland and forest petering into bare, boulder-strewn peaks.

Inside the air-conditioned car the atmosphere hung heavy with a slumbrous anger that warned her not to intrude with further words upon the mood of a man whose emotions were ravaged, an arrogant *fidalgo* smarting from the unaccustomed sting of lacerated pride. So she remained silent, trying to adjust to a dream turned nightmare, a dream that could have become blissful reality had fate not decided to intervene in the shape of the overbooking of Majorcan hotels, resulting in Kath and her husband having to settle for an alternative holiday in Portugal. One quirk of providence had made a shambles of her life, had turned the god she had worshipped into a devil, and herself into a plaything in the hands of blind chance!

Long before they reached it, the Castelo da Seteais was a landmark on the horizon, a barbaric Moorish fortress, its walls shaded from gold to ochre, perched high on top of a hill. Jade sat rooted as the car swept through an imposing archway and came to a halt inside a tiled courtyard housing a long, narrow pond hedged with myrtles that cast green shadow over a mirror-calm surface reflecting six marble columns, slim as tent-poles, supporting arches white and delicate as lace upon their carved capitals. There was a look of tender virginity about the patio nestling like a bride in need of protection beneath the towering warrior wall.

She had been too busy falling in love to give much thought to the background of the man who had blended into Lisbon society with the ease of one who took sybaritic pleasures in his stride, but as she stood in the awesome shadow of the castle built by Moorish lords she began, with a twinge of fear, to suspect that he was a man who kept his life in two watertight compartments, one in which he embraced the cultured ways of his gracious Portuguese ancestors, and another about which she could only vaguely guess but which she felt certain

had some connection with curved scimitars being
brandished aloft by fierce warriors; the arched necks
of Arab stallions stomping impatiently against the
pull of a bridle; the jangle of harness and weapons
borne by a cavalcade of returning marauders clattering under the same archway through which she
and Diego had just entered.

When he slammed shut the door of the car she
jerked, expecting to see slaves come running, but
although a servant flung open one half of a huge
brass-studded door and waited at the top of a flight
of steps to greet them, he was stooped, elderly, and
obviously Portuguese.

'This, Afonso, is Dona Jade, your new ... mistress.' Diego hesitated. 'Would you please show her
to her room now and attend to the luggage later?'

Afonso did not speak, but acknowledged her presence with a bow before indicating that she should
follow him. Jade turned a pleading look upon
Diego; for some reason she felt reluctant to step
alone inside the Castle of Seven Sighs. Whose
sighs ...? And for what had they sighed? Instinc-
tively she sensed that she was about to join the
ranks of women who had mourned their lack of
liberty; yearned for freedom from bondage; women
who had been lonely, frightened, left mostly ignored—who had loved with all their hearts and
gained nothing but contempt in return.

'Aren't you coming ...?' she gulped.

'No, Miss High and Mighty, I am not,' he jeered,
his blue eyes hooded as a hawk's. ' "Haste is of the
devil," Mohammed wrote. You must school your
heart to patience, Oh Bride of Eagerness, until your
master is ready!'

His Moorish salaam, his strange choice of expression, had been used deliberately to alarm her, Jade told herself as, crimson-cheeked, she hurried in Afonso's wake through rounded arcades and wide, pointed doorways, her heels upon marble floors echoing the frantic tapping of her heartbeats.

The room into which Afonso ushered her was flooded with light pouring through narrow arched windows framed in white stucco moulded into the shapes of flowers and seashells. From somewhere in the distance floated the sound of water tinkling softly as rain into a fountain, and as she stepped towards the window to admire the far-distant *veiga*, a lush green plain, a flock of white doves rose into flight and began circling lazily around two golden-domed minarets.

Feeling she had stepped from reality into the Arabian Nights, she toured her magnificent bedroom with its ceiling of carved wood, sculpted walls, and wardrobes with thick wooden doors carved inside and out with delicate leaves and abundant flowers. Set in a niche was a dressing table and above it a mirror, its gilded frame supported on the arms of naked, curly-haired nymphs. On a raised dais stood a huge divan, its cover of white and silver brocade strewn with brilliant green, gold, blue and purple silk cushions, and overhead a cloud of white net falling downward into the clutches of four gold-tasselled cords.

When Afonso quietly closed the door behind him she slumped down on to the divan, too stunned with misery to try to contain the flow of scalding tears that burst like a dam from pain-green eyes to flood, unchecked, down waxen cheeks.

Man is a moon with his dark side hidden! Diego

was now all darkness, his merry eyes and teasing smile eclipsed by the mist of anger and mistrust that had begun as a wisp of suspicion, then increased in density to become a glowering, tempestuous cloud. But as Jade suffered her own private maelstrom her tears stemmed not from fear but from regret—this had promised to be the happiest day of her life, the day when she was to have been swept in the arms of her husband to new, heavenly heights. But the man who had dismissed her from his presence with contempt was no longer an adoring suitor anxious to give pleasure, but more of a slit-eyed desert cheetah, the animal that attacked only when provoked but who, when wounded, was more dangerous than a leopard.

Her well of tears had long since run dry by the time Afonso appeared with her luggage, rousing her from her stupor.

'If you will permit the intrusion, *senhora*, I will send for a maid to unpack your suitcases.'

'Not just now, Afonso,' she waved a dissenting hand, keeping her tear-stained face averted.

'As you wish, *senhora*.' He made to withdraw. 'There is a bell at your bedside with which you may summon a servant should there be anything you need.'

'Thank you,' she acknowledged tightly, made uncomfortable by the man's unnerving suavity. 'What ... what time is dinner?'

'Meals are served according to my master's wishes. He has not yet intimated when he will be prepared to eat, but it will be a simple matter to have a snack served to you in your room if you are feeling hungry?'

'No, thank you,' she declined hastily, appalled

by the very thought of food, 'I was merely trying to establish a time to start dressing.'

'Usually the Senhor prefers to dine late.' She sensed his deprecating shrug, and hated the smooth urbanity with which he concluded, 'But there is always the possibility that he might wish to retire early, therefore it might be wise to begin your preparations now rather than be forced to keep him waiting.'

Made to feel like a *houri* being warned against incurring the wrath of her master, Jade mustered sufficient dignity to dismiss him coolly. 'Very well, you may go now.'

Her bathroom was a symphony in cream and gold, with scented bathsalts in crystal jars and piles of thick, deep crimson towels. Nevertheless, she was not tempted to linger; her mind was upon her next confrontation with Diego and the vital importance of reaching some sort of understanding. With this end in mind, she prepared carefully, choosing a dress in his favourite shade of blue, leaving her hair unpinned, sweeping down past her shoulders, because he loved the silken feel of it between his fingers, loved to bury his lips deep in its fragrant mass.

Because her mother had always impressed upon her that an attractively made-up face was as essential to beauty as seductive scent, shining hair, and a sweet breath, she selected her make-up with equal care, rejecting her usual tinted foundation in favour of a colourless fluid which, because it contained no oil, would not melt beneath the powder she filmed on top of it with a soft brush. She then applied eyeshadow to each lid, a shade hovering between blue and green that adapted in the manner of a chameleon both to the blue of her dress and the deep green of her eyes. Pink-tinted lip gloss and a spray of light cologne was all that was needed before she was ready to slip into a dress breathing romance out of every finely pleated fold. The gossamer chiffon hugged one shoulder and left the other completely bare, a tantalising creation, revealing and concealing at one and the same time, the perfect choice for a bride shy of making advances yet eager to co-operate.

As she bent to slide her foot into a sandal that was no more than a spike-heeled sole held in position by silver and blue strapping that bound across her toes, then coiled upwards, snaking three times around her ankle, before terminating in a diamanté serpent's head, she saw that Di's letter had slipped unnoticed to the floor. Without giving it much thought, she picked it up and popped it inside her evening bag before crossing over to a mirror to examine her appearance.

Her dress looked perfect, her hair shone as if silvered by moonbeams, her skin was flawless, her expression calm—only eyes mirroring her thoughts reflected nervous apprehension.

'No woman can be beautiful who can be false! How forcibly you disprove that theory, *cara*. At this moment you remind me of a slim blue candle with a head of silver flame.' As stealthily as he had entered, Diego strode up behind her and bent to crush his lips against the alabaster skin of her bared shoulder.

The shock of his unexpected appearance was transcended by fear when she saw sparks in the depths of his eyes threatening to flare into passionate flame. She shuddered from the thought of being taken by hands that were sliding with careless intimacy along the curve of her hip and a slim length of thigh.

'Please don't, Diego,' she choked, jerking her shoulder out of reach of his searing mouth.

His reaction was swift. Savagely he swung her round to face his dark mockery. *'Please don't, Diego ...!'* he mimicked, then jerked her close to growl down into her stricken face: 'No need to pretend any longer that you are a simple child cast adrift in a world of strangers, no need to act the part of a sensitive, easily-bruised puritan, or to imitate clear green honesty when you spin your honeyed lies—for we both know, don't we, Jade, that you are a mercenary schemer who aimed high and achieved all that she had ever wanted!' His fingers grasped her hair to twist and pull her forward until her face was just a terrifying inch from his thunderous scowl. 'You sought wealth, position, and the security of marriage—now that you have them, *be prepared to pay!'*

Lashed to his chest with arms of steel, her throat blocked with terror, she stared at the hard mouth lowering towards her, then closed her eyes, unable to bear the sight of hard dislike that had chiselled his features into a mask of stone. A sigh caught in her throat as she prepared to suffer the price of his pain, blood pounded in her ears, making her only vaguely aware of a rap upon her bedroom door and Afonso's polite request that he might enter. She felt Diego's hold slacken, sensed his slight hesitation, then as awareness dawned took immediate advantage by calling loudly as a plea:

'Enter, Alfonso, *por favor* ...!'

She heard Diego's hiss of frustration but felt no resistance when she jerked a yard of space between them. He spun away from her side as Afonso entered, but his servant ignored Jade and addressed his master's rigid back.

'*Desculpe, senhor*, I was not aware of your presence,' he paused, looking uncomfortable, then as if anxious to be absolved of blame, he continued: 'At the Senhora's request I came to inform her that dinner is now ready to be served.'

'Thank you, Afonso,' she rushed to seize the lifeline he had thrown, 'the Senhor and I are quite ready. Please lead the way and we will follow.'

CHAPTER EIGHT

THE Mauresque design of the exterior of the Castelo was emphasised in the dining-room bathed in a soft glow cast by copper lamps hung low to create an oasis of light around the table, leaving the rest of the room shrouded in shadows mysterious as the desert, through which Jade caught a glimpse of woven wall hangings and plants and flowers set in Arabic *braseros*.

Two places had been set, one at the head and the other at the foot of a table so long she realised that she and Diego would almost have to shout in order to carry on a conversation. Diego, however, seemed quite unconcerned by their state of isolation and, leaving Afonso to assist her into her chair, he took his own place at the head of the table.

With some trepidation she eyed the array of silver cutlery that had been laid out for her use. Obviously, it was to be a meal of many courses, one of the leisurely affairs so beloved of the Portuguese, who believed in embellishing each meal with the piquant sauce of wit and brilliant conversation. She glanced along the length of white lace tablecloth with its centrepiece of flowers forming a lake around an assured, gleaming silver swan; at its bowls of fruit, dishes of condiments and range of crystal glasses, trying to gauge Diego's mood, then quickly averted her eyes when she met a look of brooding somnolence—the heavy-lidded, calcu-

lating look of one who, though recently outma-
noeuvred, is confident of victory.

Either he did not notice, or he was not interested
enough to comment on the fact that she merely
toyed with each course, eating hardly any of the
food set in front of her by Afonso, who hovered
between the two of them, a silent, expressionless
spectre at the feast. Diego, however, seemed in excellent appetite, working his way through from
gazpacho to the *queijo de azeitao*, a ewe's milk
cheese which, when Jade sampled a crumb, she
found surprisingly pleasant. She had just reached
the conclusion that the long, silent meal had been
designed as part of her punishment when to her
infinite relief Diego waved a dissenting hand in
response to Afonso's offering of fruit, pushed his
chair back from the table and rose to his feet.

'Serve coffee in the *sala de extar*, if you please,
Afonso.' He picked up a plate and selected from
the fruit dish a cluster of strange-looking fruits,
small yellow globes attached in clusters to barky
stalks. '*Nesperas*,' he replied in response to her enquiring look, 'Eve's apples! It is said that they are
the original apples from the garden of Eden, one
of which Eve used to tempt Adam to forfeit his
paradise. As a true daughter of Eve, you cannot
help but enjoy them.'

A mocking smile played around his mouth as he
led her into a small, intimate *sala* that had an un-
broken range of plump, cushioned divan lining
three of its walls. A handwoven carpet covering
most of the tiled floor was dotted with stools and
low, brass-topped tables. A filigree lamp inset with
coloured glass spread beams of jewelled light, en-

closing them within a rainbow of soft radiance. From somewhere out of sight music was being piped into the room, a combination of guitar and zither playing a melody so throbbing and unrestrainedly sentimental it acted like a warning upon her over-wrought nerves.

That Diego wished them to be left completely alone and uninterrupted was made obvious when he dismissed Afonso while he was in the act of setting coffee cups on to one of the low tables.

'Thank you, Afonso, we will serve ourselves. You may retire now, if you wish, I shan't need you any more tonight.'

Without flickering an eyelash Afonso bowed, then withdrew, his mask-like expression causing Jade to shiver.

'Doesn't he ever smile?' she burst out impulsively once the door had closed behind him.

Diego gave a short laugh. 'I'm afraid he doesn't betray many signs of having received his share of the inheritance that is supposedly the due of all my countrymen: the three gifts of laughter, song and sun.'

Made nervous by the sultry ambience building up inside the room, she clutched at the conversational lifeline. 'And what about Portuguese women, have they no legacy of gifts?'

He sat next to her on the divan, looking relaxed and handsome in a dinner jacket that fitted sleek as a sealskin across wide shoulders and a pristine shirt with diamond-studded cuffs which as he reached for his coffee cup were caught by the over-head light, so that their hard glint was reflected in his eyes.

'Indeed yes, gifts that are graded according to age. From birth to twelve: innocence; from twelve to twenty-five: an amorous nature; from twenty-five to thirty: the falsity of Judas. What age are you?' he enquired so casually Jade fell neatly into his trap.

'Twenty,' she replied absently, then stiffened when his arm snaked around her shoulders.

'Then shall we discover, sweet Judas,' he murmured with his eyes upon her quivering mouth, 'whether or not you have been blessed with the same gift as your amorous Portuguese contempories?'

His kiss was swift as a snake bite, but the antidote was the willingness with which she accepted the poisonous jab, the shy eagerness with which she returned his venom with sweetness. Her yearning for a return of the love they had shared in Lisbon, those snatched moments of ecstasy during which they had pledged deep and abiding love, forced from her a response that took him by surprise. He had struck, poised for resistance, only to be vanquished by a pair of loving arms.

'Diego,' she whispered, her dress fluttering like the wings of a pale blue butterfly as she clung to his unresponsive frame, 'I love you so much—please, *please*, listen while I try to clear up our misunderstanding.'

She closed her eyes and prayed for his tense body to relax, for the hard hands that held her to stroke, soft as velvet, against her cheek.

She thought she had lost when he eased her upright until she was staring into his grave, frowning face.

'If you are about to dig another hole for me to fall into,' he accused harshly, 'then remember that it was you who fell into the last one!'

'I've always been honest with you,' she gulped, keeping her gaze steady, 'if I mellowed the truth a little it was only to make it more tolerable to myself. Certainly I didn't set out deliberately to deceive you, but when your mother began jumping to conclusions I didn't contradict her because, so far as I was concerned, my fairytale holiday had to end with a return to England written into the last chapter. I hadn't dared to look beyond that! Which is why I was so shocked when you asked me to marry you—if you remember, I did try to refuse,' she choked, 'but you wouldn't take no for an answer! Would I have turned down your offer so often were I the adventuress you accused me of being?' she charged desperately.

'Perhaps—if you were working on the premise that rejection makes a man keener,' he countered dryly, yet with a lack of harshness she found encouraging. 'The Arabs have a saying: *"A hair, perhaps, divides the false and the true,"*' he admitted soberly, 'in which case, you had better begin at the beginning, but bear in mind, Jade, that in order to deviate from the truth one needs to possess an exceptionally good memory!'

Feeling that she had been placed very definitely on probation, she began faltering her life story, outlining a childhood made happy by a mother's determination to heap upon her only child every privilege that money could buy. Lightly, she touched upon the hours she had spent in her mother's salon learning the art of cultivating beauty, hesitating only when she began relating the circumstances of her mother's death and the consequent change in her own life style.

'Not until after my mother's death did I discover that her enthusiastic plans for my future had led to her taking out a second mortgage on our home and on the salon. Naturally,' she sighed, saddened by the recollection, 'once all debts had been paid there wasn't a penny left over, and as I hadn't a relative in the world the State had no option but to take me into care.'

She tensed, then began churning inwardly when she felt the touch of his hand upon her shoulder, a gentle, erasing caress of the tender skin his mouth had earlier punished. She had to draw in a deep, steadying breath before she was able to continue.

'The authorities were kind in their way, but with so many children in their care they had to be impartial, treating me in exactly the same way as the others, which is why, although I'd had some grounding in the beauty business, I was found employment in a factory.'

'You could have turned the job down, struck out on your own ...?' he suggested quietly.

'And probably would have done,' she agreed, 'had it not been for Di.'

'Ah! The friend with whom you shared a flat— the one you so desperately missed at our wedding?'

'Yes,' she nodded, blinking back tears, 'the one who persuaded me to spend a holiday in Portugal and who must therefore take responsibility for throwing us together in the first place.' Trying to sound bright but failing dismally, she told him, 'So now you know the origin of my detestable nick-

name—Miss High and Mighty—and also the circumstances behind Kath's joking reference to my
marrying for money.'

'That's all it was—a joke?' he insisted, still wary
of being deceived.

'Just that and nothing more,' she assured him
simply, begging with her eyes to be believed.

There was no lightning change to a mood of
reconciliation. For once Diego's assurance seemed
shaken as pride and doubt struggled with a longing
to be convinced that the girl whose lovely, innocent
face and shy insecurity had stormed his heart was
not a mercenary schemer who had manipulated his
emotions towards her own ends.

It said much for her power of attraction that the
man who had inherited all the proud intolerance of
savage Moorish lords did not immediately react
with scorn but hesitated, raking her pale, serious
face with eyes dark with lingering doubt.

As calmly as she was able she withstood his silent
inquisition, willing a return of trust, of devotion,
of the leaping desire which, in the two weeks preceding their marriage, had threatened them both
with ecstatic insanity. As if in sympathy with their
mood, the music in the background drifted into a
fado melody, sad, wistful cadences that echoed her
heartache when softly she whispered:

'Why are you finding it so difficult to believe
that I love you, Diego? Your eyes must tell you
that I'm wearing no mask, in your heart you must
know that my devotion is permanent as the rock
upon which your *castelo* is built, not fluid and
changeable as the sea. Continue judging me if you
must,' tears glistened in her eyes, 'but when you

pass sentence, try to remember that my crime was one of foolishness rather than of sin.'

'Don't cry, *namorada*!' With a gentle finger he brushed away the tears trembling on her lashes. 'Tears leave scars on a wounded heart—I want my wife to remain perfect.'

Gold-spiked lashes flew upwards to search his sombre features for signs of forgiveness. 'Oh, my darling,' she burst shakily, 'how deeply I regret spoiling our wedding day!'

Through a mist of tears she saw his stern mouth soften into lines of tenderness. 'The blame is not yours alone, *querida*.' Gently he pulled her forward until her bright head was cushioned upon his chest, his lips soothing her throbbing temple. 'Some maintain that in order to achieve ultimate pleasure one must first endure pain—just as an interval in the shadows bestows twice as much warmth upon the sun.'

Shaken by their brush with disaster, they were content to hasten slowly towards the happiness they had so nearly lost. With music as a soothing salve and subdued lighting to hide any lingering quiver of misgiving, they rested in each other's arms, happy, for the moment, to appease rising passion with an exchange of tender kisses, casual caresses, and softly-murmured endearments, serenely conscious that the warmth they shared was destined to flare into passionate flame.

But sooner than she had imagined possible, Jade discovered that tenderness was not enough, so to ease her inner quivering she began slowly loosening Diego's tie and unbuttoning his shirt until she was able to slide her hand over his heart. Conscious of his amused assessment, she blushed, but continued shyly to stroke his warm skin until its smoothness was disturbed by a slight roughness beneath her fingertips. Curious, she pushed his shirt aside, searching for a reason, and discovered a tattoo, a slim crescent moon pulsating in time with his heartbeats.

'Oh ...!' She expelled a surprised breath. 'I would never have thought you agreeable to having your body ornamented with barbaric symbols.'

'That, my brazen dove,' he mocked her sudden rise of colour, 'is no mere ornament, but was endured as a guide for your benefit.'

'For *my* benefit ...?'

'In order that you may recognise me instantly when we come together in the hereafter,' he confirmed with a depth of sincerity she found amazing.

'But surely,' she fought an impulse to shrink from the primitive mark, 'tattooing is the doubtful privilege of the barbarian, a thing most civilised people consider distasteful?'

'The Moors were part of a cultured society long before most Europeans,' he told her lightly, but with eyes watchful behind narrowed lids. 'They have preserved much of the delicate magic of life, and being proud of their race they identify each person belonging to their tribe by the body markings indicating high caste. To them, a man without a tattoo is an outcast and of no account in the tribe either in this world or the next.'

'But you're not a Moor!' she protested sharply, her wide eyes betraying a flicker of unnameable fear.

His shout of laughter might have been a deliberate ploy to allay her fears, but there was no pretence about the eagerness with which he pulled her close, nor about the hunger of his lips when they pressed hard down upon hers, obliterating further feeble questions.

His pounce was so swift and sudden that the small evening bag looped around her wrist was jerked open, spilling her lipstick on to the tiled part of the floor. Its clattering noise broke his absorption, and with a crooked smile of apology he released her, then stooped to pick it up. But as he was replacing it in her bag he hesitated, his fingers exploring the wad of paper crackling in its depths.

'They told me you had received a letter from England this morning,' he approved, withdrawing the pages of closely-written script. 'I presume it was sent by your friend Di—may I read it?'

'No!' The protest was jerked from between cold, set lips. 'It ... it's personal,' Jade stumbled in reply to his surprised look of enquiry.

'Too personal for even a husband to share?' he queried.

At the coolness of his tone her heart plummeted. Was this to be the pattern of their existence—smooth on the surface, but with an undercurrent of suspicion running always underneath?

'Normally I wouldn't object to your reading any of my letters,' she assured him desperately, lifting a hand to her aching throat, 'but before you read Di's I would prefer that you first of all meet her in person so you can begin to understand the foibles and recognise the prejudices that are a result of the unkind way that life has treated her. She's a lovable, very wonderful person, but you would never recognise her as such from her thoughtlessly penned, hurriedly scrawled letters. So, please, Diego ...' she held out a shaking hand, 'give it back to me.'

He speared her with a long, hard stare, then to her agonised dismay began slowly and deliberately to unfold the incriminating pages.

Defeated, Jade slumped back against the divan and closed her eyes, too disheartened even to feel bitter about a fate that had once again snatched happiness from her grasp just as her hands were about to close around it. This time, she knew there would be no hope of reprieve, no second chance to undo the harm caused by casual, teasing references which at the first moment of reading she had skipped impatiently past, but which now returned in force to emblazon Di's messages upon the forefront of her mind.

Darling, clever Jade ... delighted that you've taken my advice and landed what sounds to be a very big fish indeed ... Just in case your Dom Diego should turn out to be a disappointment— and let's face it, past reports seem to indicate that many foreigners do—make certain that you're financially secure well before any crunch that might eventually come ... Wasn't it clever of me to insist upon your booking into a first class hotel? ... If ever you feel tempted to regret the ditching of romantic idealism, bear in mind that, though flowers may be sweeter-smelling, vegetables make much better soup!

'*Que diabo!*' Diego hissed the words through clenched teeth.

Though expected, the fierceness of the imprecation jerked her eyes open wide. His eyes were storm-black; his expression murderous! Involuntarily, she cringed from a threatened storm of words—but they did not come. Too angry to speak, he plucked her from the couch and strode with demented strides out of the *sala*, heading in the direction of her room.

Terror such as she had never before experienced blocked inside her throat any screams which would, in any case, have been abortive inside an isolated Moorish castle surrounded by battle-scarred walls and filled with purposely deaf servants.

She managed only one protesting moan when, in the privacy of her bedroom, he ripped her butterfly dress to shreds and threw her on to the divan.

What followed afterwards was the onset of an oft-recurring nightmare during which the talons of a vengeful hawk dug deep into her soft skin to soar her upwards to dark, terrifying heights of tempestuous emotion, before releasing her with a suddenness that jarred her aching body.

Then came the pain of his final contemptuous rejection. 'The discovery that you are a virgin is an unexpected bonus,' he snarled. 'I trust, nevertheless, that you are sufficiently experienced to take whatever precautions are necessary to ensure that you never bear any child of mine!'

Then she was left alone to sob away the agony.

CHAPTER NINE

THE next morning Jade's breakfast was served to
her in her room, borne on a tray by the inscrutable
Afonso who left it by her bedside and then silently
withdrew.

She had slept hardly at all during the long,
anguish-filled night in which she had striven to find
excuses for Diego's behaviour.

If, at first meeting, she had been honest about her
background would such a situation have arisen?
If she had rushed to show him Di's letter, might
they have laughed together over her friend's curious
prejudices?

But though she had tried hard to exonerate him
from blame forgiveness would not come. His treatment of herself had been callous, insensitive, utterly
barren of love—he had taken her as an Arab would
take a *houri*, showing as little concern for her used
body and bruised emotions as any plundering
Moorish barbarian. Yesterday, a fire had blazed—
today she was left alone to rake over the ashes!

Wearily, she heaved herself up on to her pillow,
intending to soothe her parched throat with some
of the coffee whose aroma was drifting from the
spout of a slender-waisted coffee pot. But as she
reached towards the tray her pain-drugged eyes
became fixed, unable to travel farther than the
silver dish full of caviar that was forming a nest
around a large, milk-white pearl. Even as she picked

up the note propped up against the dish she knew that its contents would be hurtful, yet she had not imagined that agony could hook so deeply into her heart as it did when dazedly she read:

Accept this pearl as the price of purity—and as a reminder of the tears that must be shed in the pursuit of wealth.

Without knocking, Diego entered her bedroom an hour later and found her sitting motionless by the window, looking out across the lush green plain. For a moment he stood, unnoticed, studying an immobility so complete that not even a tendril of hair stirred against the tender nape of her neck, not a quiver disturbed the symmetry of lips that mere hours ago had been punished by the crush of his passionate anger. Even the bodice of her leaf-green dress remained still, as if the heart beneath had become petrified.

'*Querida amor!*' he drawled. 'How are you feeling this morning?'

The confused start, the rise of colour, that he had always associated with innocence, did not materialise; instead she turned a pale but composed face towards him and even managed the ghost of a tremulous smile.

'Quite well, thank you, Diego,' she replied steadily, looking almost kindly upon her husband of a few hours towering relaxed and conscienceless, his hands thrust into the pockets of denim slacks, his skin contrasting brown as a nut against a white tee shirt, his black hair damp, twisted into dark spirals after a recent shower.

He frowned, taken aback by the lack of condemnation in her eyes, unable to guess how grateful she was, how serene in the knowledge that after she had been forced to the very nadir of misery there was nothing he could do to hurt her by comparison.

'I thought,' he eyed her narrowly, 'that we might take a drive. Some sea air should bring back the colour to your cheeks.'

'That would be nice,' she agreed politely, rising to stand obediently waiting, her hands clasped loosely in front of her.

'There's no need to adopt the attitude of a schoolgirl,' he accused irritably, his cheekbones highlighted by a slow rise of colour which, in anyone other than Dom Diego da Luz Pereira da Silves, she might have suspected had its origin in discomfiture. 'Didn't they teach you anything other than conformity at your convent school?'

'They taught me about the devil,' she replied simply, 'and I know now that everything they said about him is true.'

It was an unusual sensation, being driven towards the coast in Diego's car knowing that somehow the tables had been turned, that the man by her side was feeling as disconcerted as she had often felt before an armour of ice had formed around her heart, rendering her blood cool, her mind blank, and her emotions non-existent.

Immune for the very first time to the reactions of the black-browed *fidalgo*, she was able to enjoy the sights of a countryside screaming summer from every available corner, every mound of earth, every crack between walls, every cultivated garden and line of pots decorating balconies and stairs bursting out a colourful, flamboyant spill of flowers. A glimpse of a sweep of firm, clean sand and brilliant blue sea prompted her to satisfy her curiosity with the question:

'Why is it that so few tourists visit your country when you possess an abundance of everything the holidaymakers seek? Why are the roads left empty, the coves as solitary as oases?'

'Because we prefer them as they are,' he told her, seeming surprised by her interest in the subject. 'Unlike the Spaniards, we are determined to avoid the exploitation of our country by foreigners. Although, in certain appropriate places, we have allowed the building of some luxury hotels and holiday playgrounds,' he admitted, 'basically, the many small fishing villages have been left undisturbed, their inhabitants concerned only with the canning and exporting of sardines and tuna fish. As tourists are mostly inedible and not worth canning, they excite very little interest.'

He parked the car in the centre of a strange and beautiful town that was split into two halves, the lower portion housing a small harbour crammed with tall, slender fishing boats and the upper perched high on top of a cliff, its buildings blessed with the choice of viewing either land, sea, sky, or all three, from its windows.

Taking Jade's hand in his, Diego led her down towards the busy fishing quarter where on a steep, stony beach four pairs of oxen were hauling a knife-prowed boat on to the shore. Miles of fishing nets formed an eye-catching trellis upon the sand where they had been left to dry in the sun and gusting wind.

'Are you feeling cold?' he asked her, sounding

solicitous, almost as if he cared. 'This wind, though warm, is responsible for the permanently raging seas that make this stretch of coast dangerous to fishermen. As you can see,' he nodded towards a covey of black-clad women, obviously fishermen's wives, 'in this area, the women are seldom out of mourning.'

'No, I'm not cold,' she replied truthfully, 'actually, I'm enjoying the feel of the wind upon my face. It seems a long time since——'

'... you were in your own country?' he finished for her. 'Already, like the Norwegian princess, are you pining for your homeland?'

'Perhaps ...' Delicately she disengaged her hand from him. 'I might pay Di a visit soon?' At the sight of his immediate frown she amended, 'Not just yet, but in a week or so, maybe—after all,' she reminded him coolly, 'it would be silly, under the circumstances, for either of us to pretend that we wouldn't welcome a break from each other's company.'

Diego halted suddenly to twirl her round to face him. 'A wife's place is by her husband's side!' he charged, turbulent as the waves hissing over the beach of shifting stones. 'So you can forget whatever contingency plans you and your friend may have concocted in the event of any separation and learn to live with your ... *disappointment*! Wherever I go, you will go, and I certainly do not choose to visit England!'

There upon a busy beach surrounded by the sight and smell of fish, long and small, plump and slim, round and straight, all set out in buckets with their heads upwards so that the pinkness of

their open mouths could provide proof of freshness,
Jade chose to ask the question that had a most important bearing upon her future. She might have
been enquiring about the time of day when, with
eyes devoid of the least flicker of interest, her mouth
without the merest trace of a quiver, she queried:

'Do you mean that even though there's not the
least chance of us ever finding happiness together
you intend to continue with this meaningless marriage?'

'I mean exactly that,' he nodded, his dark eyes
projecting an hauteur which in the past had blud-
geoned her small amount of assurance into utter
confusion, but which this time was met with a composure that defeated him. 'But don't worry,' he
grated, incensed by her puzzling serenity, 'though
I was not aware at the time of our marriage that
you were entering into it as you would a bargain,
I shall see to it that all your ambitions are achieved.
You will get your furs, your jewellery, all the trap-
pings of wealth, and in return ...' he hesitated,
his eyes clouded by a memory that seemed to be
inflicting some sort of pain.

'Yes, Diego ...?' she urged softly, 'what will you
receive in return—a woman without a heart, one
who is incapable of feeling even hatred or contempt? Even your legendary king of the Algarve
was rendered so frustrated by his ice-maiden he had
to agree to letting her go—and besides that,' she
reminded him gently, 'this is the twentieth century,
and if I should decide to leave there would be
nothing you could do to prevent me.'

A gust of wind caught his hair, tossing a dark
lock on to his forehead, lending him the look of

a reckless pirate, one of those who had sailed from Morocco to this very coast in order to pillage, plunder and rape. In just the same way as his, their eyes must have reflected the anticipation of the chase; their determination to conquer, their callous indifference to inflicting hurt.

'I suffer no misgivings on either score, sweet Judas,' he mocked, sending her a smile that would have chilled, had her senses not already been frozen. 'In the first instance—ice must inevitably melt, and in the second,' he puzzled her, 'even captured animals are wary of escaping into unfamiliar territory.'

As if he was really concerned that she should enjoy their outing, he let the subject drop and began exerting a strength of charm that Jade appreciated for its absence of strain, but which left her emotionally cold. She had remembered to bring her camera, so he began pointing out various items of local interest and, as they neared the fish quay, singled out the busy *varinas* as being colourful photographic subjects.

'These remarkably statuesque women are said to be of Phoenician origin,' he told her. 'Because they and their menfolk have held racially aloof, intermarriage with other races being very rare, they have retained the same physical characteristics as their ancestors—long-limbed, muscular, yet beautifully proportioned bodies, and dark, passionate eyes.'

Jade watched as one of the girls plucked out of the air a heavy basket of fish that had been flung in her direction. She emptied the contents into a flat tray, then threw back the weighty box with as little effort as she would have used playing a game of tennis. On the quayside, other women wearing haloes of what seemed to be plaited straw on top of their headsquares were scurrying in various directions, each with a heavy box of sardines balanced on top of her head. All around the fish peddlers' peculiar cry—half flamenco, half yodel—could be heard.

Jade was clicking madly away, with Diego an amused spectator, when two merry-eyed boys planted themselves foursquare in front of her.

'*Senhora*,' an impudent voice addressed her, 'would you like to take our pictures?'

'I would,' she smiled, taking a step back to get them both in focus.

'In that case,' there was silence for a moment while they grinned and posed, 'give us both some *escudos* for ice-cream!'

Diego looked outraged by the blatant blackmail, but Jade found their cheek irresistible.

'Please, Diego,' she laughed into his frowning face, 'I know such an attitude shouldn't be encouraged, but they're such *little* boys, so perhaps, just this once ...?'

'*Meu Deus!*' He shrugged his despair. 'You are encouraging them into a life of corruption!' Yet even while he scolded, his hand was delving into his pocket.

The atmosphere between them was companionable as they left the quayside behind them and began ascending the steep road leading to the upper half of the town.

'I know of a restaurant that serves excellent *esparadate*, are you ready for some lunch?'

Surprisingly, Jade discovered that she was. Just a few hours ago she would have been ready to swear that she would never enjoy a meal again, but the combination of exercise and an invigorating sea breeze had made her conscious of a void that had its origin in hunger.

They had almost reached the restaurant of his choice when she stopped with a cry of admiration, entranced by a display of unusual objects in a shop window.

'Haven't you heard of the figs of Portugal?' Diego queried across her shoulder.

'Figs?' She swung round, wide-eyed. 'They can't possibly be edible!'

'I was not referring to the fig fruit,' he laughed down at her, 'but to omens designed to ward off the evil eye. Almost every girl in Portugal wears such a "fig" somewhere about her person. Come to think of it,' his voice developed a drawl, 'I can think of no other girl more in need than yourself of a charm against ill-fortune. Come,' he grasped her by the elbow to urge her through the shop doorway, 'obviously, for one who treats life as a lottery, we must purchase a slice of luck.'

Jade tried not to dwell upon his barbed remark as the jeweller set out upon his counter row upon row of 'fig' amulets, beautifully carved ivory hands adorned with gold fingernails, gold wedding ring, and a gold bracelet shackled around a slender, graceful wrist. There was such a variety of size and quality she could not make up her mind which one to choose, but finally she settled for the tiniest, perfect in every detail, fashioned to be worn around the neck suspended from a fine gold chain.

Not until she caught a glimpse of avaricious satisfaction in the jeweller's eyes did she begin vaguely to suspect that she had chosen the most expensive item in his collection, but by that time it was too late to change her mind.

'Don't bother to wrap it up,' Diego instructed when the shopkeeper began arranging the charm in a presentation box, 'my wife will wear it now.'

The touch of his fingers was warm against the nape of her neck when he adjusted the minute catch, yet she shivered, chilled by his dry response to her involuntary protest that she had not meant to choose the most expensive. Though obviously, to him, cost was of no consequence, he had been unable to resist the sarcastic jeer:

'I believe you, *cara*—as I would believe a farmer insisting upon his honesty even as minnows were swimming in his milk pail.'

Nevertheless, he did not allow the incident to cast a blight upon their meal, but engaged her in teasing conversation while they enjoyed a delicious iced soup, and prodded from her a gasp of outrage when, after eating with relish a portion of *esparadate*, the restaurant's speciality, he calmly informed her:

'You have just experienced your first taste of smoked swordfish, Jade, how did you like it?'

As she pictured in her mind's eyes the huge, ugly fish she had seen arranged in the fishmarket with their wicked, sharp snouts pointing high into the air, her stomach rebelled. 'Oh, no! Why didn't you warn me?' she gasped, reaching for her glass to gulp down a mouthful of the *vin rosé* she had insisted upon choosing even though Diego had scoffed that it was a drink for schoolgirls at their first party. She, however, found it alarmingly potent, a fact to which she attributed the swimming of her senses when her eyes caught his twinkling glance as she glared across the table.

'I must remember that you are averse to eating the unknown and the unusual if ever we are called upon to feast with my Arab friends,' he grinned. 'Basically, their meals are made of mutton and honoured guests are invariably given the eyes of the sheep.'

Jade stared, horrified. 'Are you deliberately trying to nauseate me?' she accused, having to resort to a second gulp of wine.

'Perhaps it was rather unkind of me,' he admitted, becoming aware of her genuine distress, 'actually you will never be called upon to sample sheep's eyes, for far from being treated as honoured guests women are seldom allowed to eat in masculine Arab company. Indeed, the only concession they make to acknowledging the presence of a woman in their midst is to send a present of fruit gathered from bushes scattered around the oasis which, carried as an amulet, enjoys a widespread reputation for preserving chastity.'

She was prepared to believe that it was a genuine slip up on his part, that he had not meant to remind her of the happenings of the previous evening, but it was impossible to hold back the shadows that clouded her eyes and impossible, because of the lump sticking in her throat, to partake of another bite of food, even another sip of wine.

She sensed that Diego was regretful of his clumsiness when without further words he settled their bill and escorted her outside, and though the

proud *fidalgo* made no effort to apologise his silence
was sufficient indication of vexation as he drove out
of the town and headed once more into the open
countryside.

He took to a main road a mile or two inland in
order to avoid the twists and turns of a deeply
indented coastline, but when shortly he cut off on
to a secondary road winding past orchards and
fields full of flowers and wild strawberries he pulled
up at the gate of an orchard to buy her a peace
offering—a glass jar full of peaches preserved in
a clear white syrup.

Her acceptance of the gift was polite but prim—
her forgiveness could not be bought either with
peaches or pearls—so with a scowl once more darkening his features he slid back into his seat and
drove on.

It was perhaps not so surprising that he should
feel tempted to punish her when, as they drove
past a small grove of cork trees, he stopped the car
when she cried out with amazement, then set out
deliberately to embarrass her.

Men had stripped the trees of their rough bark,
baring a slender, milk-white trunk under a short
skirt of leaves. The sinuous-looking, flesh-tinted
trees bore a strange resemblance to a chorus line
of nudes tossing green, full-skirted dresses over their
heads.

'It would not do for an inhibited man to become
lost in such a wood at dusk,' he growled, his wicked
eyes enjoying her slow rise of colour. Then, taking
slight pity on her embarrassment, he explained,
'For four months after stripping the trunks remain
white, then from four to eight months they turn
red, and from eight months to a year they adopt

black tones. 'Myself,' he reverted to sardonic humour, 'I prefer a delightful silky skin with the ivory tenderness one associates with a nude Saxon maid.'

Jade's cheeks were still flaming as they travelled through an attractive valley with brightly coloured cottages outstanding amongst slopes nursing fig, almond and olive groves. She had a splitting headache, caused either by tense embarrassment or by the heavy aroma hanging in the atmosphere, the smell of newly-pressed grapes—fermenting almost immediately in the heat—that was drifting in an intoxicating cloud from a nearby winery.

By the time the road began plunging downwards towards a beach fringed by sparkling blue sea the ache had become almost unbearable, so when Diego parked the car she tossed off her sandals and ran across the firm sand of the deserted cove to paddle barefoot in the sea. Once more his presence was beginning to impinge upon her nerves, senses she had thought permanently cauterised were once more stirring into life, transmitting urgent signals at the sight, the sound, the nearness of him. But the lap of waves around her feet did nothing to cool the fever of a mind churning with resurrected memories, memories of a bruising mouth, a sensuous touch, and biting, heartbreaking words.

There was something threatening about the way in which, when Diego caught up with her, he clasped forceful fingers around her wrist to hold her close to his side as together they sauntered slowly along the curve of beach, splashing through the waves.

'There is a grotto in the cliffs over there,' he

directed with a nod. 'Would you like to see inside of it?'

Distrusting the too-casual tenor of his voice, the pantherish tension of his limbs, she began a shaky refusal. 'No, thank you, if you don't mind, I'd like to go home now, I've had enough of sunshine for one day.'

'But you must,' he insisted silkily, drawing her to a halt opposite a small opening in the cliffs. 'It won't take a minute, and inside it is all coolness and shade. Come,' his dark eyes seemed flecked with flame, 'it is an experience that should not be missed.'

The cave did, indeed, prove to be worth a visit. Though tiny as a tomb, its walls had been twisted and curled by the sea into forms identifiable as bunches of fruit and vegetables and other artistic designs sculpted by nature out of colourful stone. The floor of firm, clean sand felt cool beneath Jade's feet, a shaded breeze feathered the heat from her skin, so that his lips felt fiery as a brand when they pressed an urgent kiss upon the nape of her neck.

'False Jade,' he murmured hoarsely, swinging her up into his arms before lowering her gently on to the sand. She saw eyes brilliant with intent lowering towards her and with a piteous moan she closed her eyes, trying to shut out the sight of reality, but unable to escape his last throaty murmur before he shut out the world.

'Deceitful wife, I doubt, despise, disapprove of you utterly—but, *Deus, how madly I desire you!*'

CHAPTER TEN

JADE was sitting in the patio protected from the sun by a small fretwork chalet filled with the pungent scent of roses rambling thickly over trelliswork to create a shaded, perfumed bower. A writing pad lay on the table in front of her, but her sightless gaze was focused upon the tree-fringed pond filled with colourful fish darting lazily between the waterlily leaves that spread a protective canopy over the surface of the water. With a pen held between limp fingers she began doodling abstract designs bearing no relation to thoughts about an uneventful week during which she had been left to her own devices.

'There is much work to catch up on,' Afonso had informed her when she had queried Diego's absence from meals. 'The Senhor's visit to Lisbon was meant to last only a few days; unforeseeable problems arose on the *quinta* when his visit was extended.'

She had felt reproved—Afonso had sounded as if he held her completely responsible both for his master's lengthy absence and for the spate of work that had arisen as a consequence.

'But surely the Senhor employs a manager, some responsible person who can be left in charge?'

'*Sim, senhora,*' he had looked pitying, already designating her a tiresome whim his master was regretting, 'but there are some important decisions that only Dom Diego can make.'

Of course, there would be, Jade had accepted dully. Diego was the kingpin around which everything revolved, the foundation stone upon which the Castelo, its estate and dependent villages rested—a monarch to whom all his subjects had pledged allegiance!

Wearily, she pushed back a heavy wave of hair from her forehead and braced slim shoulders aching from a weight of desolation that was increasing day by day, hour by lonely hour. During the first half of the week she had spent her time exploring the Castelo and its superbly-tended gardens laced with lakes that were home to magnificent black swans whose proud arrogance might have been inherited from their owner. She had walked entranced past rock gardens, waterfalls spannel by ornamental bridges, flamboyant shrubs and tall trees splashing shade upon a carpet of flowers spread out beneath them. Inside the Castelo she had wandered through rooms filled with gold and silver plate, priceless rugs and porcelain too fragile to dare to reach out and touch; she had studied magnificent views of the countryside from each of the many windows, even spotting from one of them old pear, apple and cherry orchards.

The exploration had left her overawed, convinced as never before that there was no niche for herself in such surroundings. Her place was back home where, with the help of the hardest and most demanding job she could find, she might manage to erase from her memory every trace of this Castle of Sighs and the man who had provoked them.

Desperately she tightened her fingers around her

pen and began writing a letter to Di, an outpouring
of words pleading for help to escape from intolerable unhappiness, words she was able to pen with
passionate frankness only because, even as she
wrote, she was aware that as she was a virtual
prisoner inside the Castelo, without access to a post-
box, they were never destined to be read.

Nevertheless, she felt great relief when she folded
the finished letter, sealed it in an envelope, and
wrote down Di's carefully memorised address. She
had just finished when a shadow fell across the
table, causing a nervous reflex that sent the pen
haywire across the face of the envelope.

'Oh!' Guilty eyes flew upwards, then softened
with relief when she recognised the intruder.
'Pedro, how you startled me!' she gasped, then
smiled encouragement at the shy young gardener's
boy whose doe-brown eyes radiating mute admiration had been her one source of comfort during
her week of solitary confinement. Every time she
had turned he had seemed to be lurking in her
shadow, ostensibly sweeping up leaves, tidying
paths, or clearing weeds from the flowerbeds, but
always with his eyes trained in her direction.

Feeling sympathy for the boy whose agony was
her own constant companion, she remarked gently,
'You look hot, would you like a drink of lemonade?'
she nodded towards an iced jugful set at the side
of the table. 'Help yourself—*sirva-se*,' she stumbled,
wishing desperately that they could communicate.

Casting a nervous glance across his shoulder, the
boy edged away. '*E muito amaval, senhora—e muito
angelico*,' he mumbled, then, seemingly appalled
by his own temerity, turned to scurry away.

'Wait! *Alto la!*' Feeling less kind, less angelic than she had ever felt in her life before, Jade grasped at a sudden, unexpected straw. Advancing towards the boy with the envelope in her out-stretched hand, she struggled with urgent, unfamiliar words. '*Faca o favor correiro esta carta?*' For a second the boy stared as if mystified by her request to post a letter, then to her joy he grabbed it from her hand, shoved it into his pocket, then quickly ran away.

Feeling elated, yet too scared to dwell upon Diego's reaction should he find out about her bid for freedom, Jade hurried up to her room, her mind furiously calculating the length of time it would take for the letter to be posted, to arrive at its destination, then how soon she might hope for a response from Di. But even this important issue took second place to amazement when she burst into her room and jerked to a halt, confronted by pile upon pile of black cardboard boxes each with a flamboyant signature scrawled in gold upon its lid.

Slowly she stepped towards the nearest pile and began easing off the topmost lid. A swathe of mauve tissue paper sighed in the draught of the lifted lid, then at the touch of her fingers fell apart to reveal the richly glowing material of a superb evening dress.

For the following two hours she was enveloped within the Thousand-and-One-Nights atmosphere of *haute couture* as she delved into box after box, too basically feminine to resist the seduction of fur-trimmed shawls, ball dresses in heavy, brilliant satins, frothing taffeta petticoats, velvet and organdie dresses, some full-skirted, some cut on the bias and caught on one shoulder, others sheathed to cling to the hips, soft as a cat's purr, tapering narrowly towards the ankles, then slashed upwards to the knee, baring a glimpse of jewelled lining and a tantalising length of limb.

Her vision had become blurred, her bedroom an Aladdin's cave filled with clothes, frogged, ruffed, sequined and embroidered, by the time she had progressed to the last box that was wider and much deeper than the rest. She knew the moment she felt the stroke of fur against her fingers that she was about to receive the ultimate accolade a rich man can bestow upon his wife—or his mistress— a full-length, pure white evening cape fashioned from mink, trimmed along cuffs, hem, and face-framing hood with a deep band of opulent fox fur.

Without bothering to try it on, she sank back on her heels, overwhelmed by Diego's generosity yet at the same time repelled by the man who combined cruelty with sensitivity of taste, whose breathtaking gifts hid premeditated insults—who had turned a cove into a shrine of passion even while plotting where best to position his knife.

Desultorily, she began tidying up the cloud of tissue paper floating around the floor, wishing it were as easy to restore order to a chaotic mind. She could have rung to summon the help of a maid, but the task of placing each gorgeous creation on a hanger before transferring it into a wardrobe was balm to her fretful hands. Once this had been achieved and the empty boxes were stacked in the passageway outside of her room for Afonso to dispose of at his leisure, she sank down upon the bed and lay with her pale hair, misty as a veil, across a jade green cushion, too hurt even to shed a tear, heartened only slightly by the knowledge that at this very moment her letter of appeal should be speeding on its way.

She must have slept, for she was startled awake by a sudden movement as a tall frame lowered itself down beside her. For a moment her sleep-drugged eyes could not focus, then gradually her vision cleared to allow her to distinguish Diego's chiselled profile, his saturnine smile. He was sitting on the edge of the bed looking healthily virile, as if a day's honest toil had agreed with him. Obviously, he had not spared the time to shower and change before seeking her reaction to his latest act of revenge; his denims were crumpled, his hair tousled, his shirt slightly stained and pungent with the heavy, heady aroma of newly-pressed grapes. Muscles sinewed as a peasant's rippled beneath bronzed skin as he reached out to touch a tendril of hair that had fallen on to her forehead.

'You sleep like a baby, *namorada*. Are you worn out with the excitement of unpacking your boxes of treasure? Tell me,' dark eyes lurked dangerously lazy behind half-closed lids, 'are you pleased with the fripperies I have chosen for you?'

'Was I meant to be pleased?' she choked, alarmed by this new powerful-peasant image. 'Don't try to deny that your aim was to humiliate, that the purpose behind your *unexpected* visit was to discover whether or not you'd succeeded!'

The bitterness that coloured her tone when she referred to his visit appalled her—she had sounded like a wife berating a neglectful husband!

Diego's quick, cynical grin was proof that he, too, had noticed.

'Have you missed me, *querida*?' he asked softly, lowering his head so close her mouth felt menaced. He had the look of a man in a mood of devilry, one pleasantly tired after a day of exertion yet lazily disposed to be entertained.

Jerking her profile out of reach of his stroking fingers, Jade rolled across the bed and jumped to her feet to put its space between them. His laughter was infuriating, yet not so much as the attitude with which he stretched his length out on her bed, propped up his head with her pillows, then crisply commanded:

'Very well, as you seem reluctant to credit me with a discerning eye, I must insist that you try on the dresses so that I can see for myself whether my judgment is faulty.'

'What, *all* of them?' she gasped.

'Why not?' he insisted silkily, complacent as a sultan in the comfort of his harem. 'Can you think of a better way to spend an idle hour? But perhaps,' his taunting eyes grew keen, 'you have an even more entertaining alternative in mind ...?'

His jeering laughter pursued her as she grabbed an armful of clothes from the wardrobe and fled behind an accommodating screen.,

As he had intended, she felt terribly self-conscious and showed it in the awkwardness with which, in response to his command, she began parading around the room. If he had studied the subject for years, he could not have come up with a more degrading form of punishment for a girl with feelings so sensitive that a cynically-twisted lip, a prolonged stare, was sufficient to inflict a wound. Yet he insisted upon her continuing with the humiliating charade, forcing her into obedience with suggestive remarks that kept the threat of retaliation hanging heavily over her downcast head.

'I'm not sure about that one,' he frowned, when she stepped from behind the screen wearing an ankle-length dress in vivid pink, its flounced skirt and off-the-shoulder neckline supplying gypsy overtones. Her knees began trembling as she walked towards him; the atmosphere inside the room was fraught and that, together with the effort she had expended parading like a mannequin for the better part of an hour, was beginning to take its toll.

'Perhaps if you wore a flower behind your ear and another tucked into your waistband ...?' he eyed her critically. 'But on the whole, I feel satisfied with my choice. Each of the dresses you have worn has in its own way acted as a perfect foil for your beauty, with the exception of this one that seems to have drawn all the colour from your cheeks.'

'I'm tired, Diego. Please, may I rest now?'

When he swung his legs from the bed and stood upright she jerked away. His mouth tightened, making his reply sound merciless.

'Not yet, not until you have worn the white fur—in that, I fancy, you will look superb. Most females possess some of the characteristics of the feline, sometimes to the point of betraying national charactistics. Spanish and Turkish women, for instance, just like their cats, are spitfires. English, French and German cats are pampered pets, but we Portuguese,' lightly he pinched her chin between his thumb and forefinger to raise her downbent head, 'although quite fond of the creatures, treat them in a nonchalant manner, leaving them to forage for their own food so that invariably they possess slim, healthy bodies.'

Jade shivered beneath his touch, comparing him in her mind with the sinuous black tom she had seen prowling the passageways of the Castelo, slant-eyed, slim-tailed, the muscles beneath its sleek skin playing as if shaped by a sculptor's hand as it stalked like a panther through its domain.

'Why do you shiver?' he asked. 'Don't you like cats?'

'Not very much,' she admitted huskily. 'I don't mind placid tabbies, but the few I've seen around here have struck me as being cold-blooded auto-crats.' *Not unlike yourself*, she could have added, but dared not.

'Which is just as it should be,' he nodded, 'con-sidering they were brought here from Arabia by the Moors and are reputed to be the reincarnation of the ancient cat deity of Egypt. But you need not cower from them, frightened sparrow, for contrary to the English belief that the black cat is the witches' chosen companion, we believe that the presence of one of them in the house will success-fully prevent the intrusion of bad spirits.'

At that moment she found the superstition hard to credit, for the atmosphere, filled with foreboding, had the effect of making her feel cowed as a per-forming animal under the threat of a trainer's whip.

Unconsciously, Diego added credence to the

simile. 'And now, Jade, the white fur! Let me see you wearing it.'

He turned his back and walked towards the window while she fumbled inside the wardrobe, resenting his insistence yet too tired and dispirited to argue. She ought to have luxuriated in the touch of its silky caress against her skin, and if the gift had been motivated by even mild affection she might have done, but it represented yet another stripe across her back, so her expression reflected inner pain when he turned round to face her.

For a long time he said nothing, but stood silently staring at features made to look even more delicate by a frame of soft, pristine fur, and at a slim form to which the supple skins had lent an unsuspected dignity.

The sound of his harshly-indrawn breath startled her, but she did not look up, not even when his voice grated:

'Whichever man decided that you were suitable only for menial work must have been blind, *namorada*, lacking emotional as well as physical perception—he must have glanced at you only long enough to tie on a label.' Suddenly he moved, to jerk her into an embrace tight enough to have tamed a tiger. Lightly he traced his lips across her brow, feathered across her cheek, then plunged to burrow deeply into her tender neck. 'Your hair has the scent of honey,' he growled, then, aggravated by her frozen stillness, he lifted his head to pierce her armour with fierce, condemning words.

'It is wrong that someone so extraordinarily beautiful should lack morals indicative of such beauty. *Look at me, innocent eyes*,' he shook her roughly,

'I *know* you are false—an enchanting cheat who can sway a man's senses without uttering a word!'

A green flash of fear widened her eyes, fear of the man whose anger seemed all the more violent because it was directed not just against her but against himself, fear of the man whose virile body was straining to contain frustration built up like a dam inside him, the man barbaric as the tribal mark he carried on his chest.

'Please, Diego,' desperation made claws of her clutching fingers, 'please leave me in peace!'

'Leave you in peace!' he hissed, black head tossing in the manner of an enraged stallion. 'Why should I? You are my wife, I have given you all you ever wanted from our marriage, therefore am I not entitled to receive my own paltry share?'

'Oh, Diego,' she whispered brokenly, her eyes glowing with unshed tears, 'do you really believe that a marriage can survive on presents of costly pearls and expensive furs?'

'So, Ice Maiden, you are not yet satisfied,' he clamped. 'Tell me what else I must provide before your frozen heart can begin to thaw?'

'Affection,' she choked, 'sympathy, and perhaps most important of all, friendship, because friendship outlives physical attraction. Without it, no marriage can mature from mere emotionalism to deep affection and mutual understanding. The strongest ties, Diego, can be those that are least vibrant.'

The jerk of a muscle in his cheeks confirmed that she had managed to touch a nerve. Hope, the small lifeless thing that had seemed condemned to life imprisonment within the Castelo's walls, stirred

anew at the sound of a voice pitched low, and
strangely gentle.

'How unfortunate it is that you are so often misjudged, sweet Jade—especially unfortunate,' his
hand snaked to his pocket to withdraw a familiar
white envelope, 'for a susceptible young boy whose
infatuation led him to risk his home, his job, and
the welfare of his widowed mother in exchange for
a look of approval from your deceivingly honest
eyes!'

The softness of his tone suddenly revealed itself
as menace, a creeping cloud threatening to smother
the life out of her. Yet self-preservation was not her
first concern, all she could think of was Pedro, the
boy whose future could be ruined in this land
where feudal conditions still prevailed.

'Don't punish Pedro because of me,' she begged,
her eyes enormous in a stricken face. 'I'm sorry
about the letter, but Pedro was in no way to blame!
I'll do anything!' In an agony of remorse she clutched his arms in an attempt to shake his rock-hard
body. 'I'll do anything at all you might ask of me,
but please, *please*, don't take your revenge on
Pedro!'

Diego took time to savour his triumph, keeping
her so long on the rack of suspense that it seemed
an eternity had passed before the first screw was
loosened.

'As you admit that the blame is entirely yours,
we must think up a punishment equivalent to the
crime,' he drawled, exercising his inherited Moorish
tyranny. Jade waited with head bowed, her numbed
mind struggling to assimilate his words. 'The sentence that most appeals to me should not prove too

difficult for one whose talent for acting becomes more obvious with each passing day. *I want you to give yourself to me.* I've grown weary of cold, emotionless kisses, of a body that responds only to force, never by inclination. It is in you to display all the earthy passion of a peasant,' he finished almost lazily. 'I have sensed it, but so far, the experience remains tantalisingly out of reach.'

She pulled away with loathing, reminded more than ever of the pantherish creature that prowled the Castelo, its back arching at every friendly approach, spitting aggression in response to every cajoling word. The reason behind his visit had become suddenly plain: he had come, with her letter in his pocket, to lounge upon her bed, to enjoy her reaction to his threatening play upon words, to subject her to a humiliating parade of worldly goods, all the time knowing that he held one last, shaming, untrumpable card.

A shudder ran through her as she stared, small face cowled like a novice, preparing to agree to his demand.

'Very well, Diego,' she whispered, 'but first I must have your promise that Pedro will not be made to suffer for my sins?'

'You have it,' he assured with a glint, holding wide his arms.

Slowly she crept into them, forced her arms slowly around his neck, then pulled his dark head down towards her. With a sigh that was almost a sob, she stood on tiptoe to crush soft lips against his hard mouth, trying to instil sweetness, making no attempt to retain her last remaining barrier, the ability to stand aloof, to lock inside her all loving responses in a way that frustrated his desire to possess her completely.

But though she projected all the fervour she found possible, Diego remained strangely unresponsive, his arms locked loosely around her waist leaden with lack of tension. Desperately, she tried harder, pressing her wraith-slim body against his unyielding trunk, forcing quivering lips to deliver a message of desire upon his daunting mouth.

She had not realised she was crying until he pushed her aside.

'Stop it, Jade!' He brushed a hand across his lips, as if he found the taste of her tears bitter, before bleakly rejecting her. 'The choice I've been given is too limited—to make love to an ice maiden is bad enough, yet it is infinitely preferable to being seduced by a nun as part of her penance!'

CHAPTER ELEVEN

As was his wont, Diego strode without knocking into Jade's bedroom the following morning. She had just finished dressing and was standing by the window looking out across the plain, wondering how to fill in the day that stretched long and wearily in front of her.

'I have to make a short business trip,' he told her, eyeing her pale beauty almost with dislike, 'and as I cannot trust you to behave while I am away, I have no alternative but to take you with me. Pack a bag with serviceable items—slacks, and tops with sleeves to protect you from the sun.' Almost as an afterthought, he cast across his shoulder as he was leaving the room, 'You'll also need a warm coat, the desert grows cold at night time.'

The desert! Jade's lips parted to eject a dozen surprised questions, but before the first one could be voiced the door had closed behind him.

Sensing from his manner that he was in an irritable, impatient mood that would not improve by being kept waiting, she hurriedly packed a suitcase with clothes she hoped would be suitable, but having not the faintest notion which clothes would be considered correct in desert terrain, she discarded chic in favour of comfort.

If only he had been more explicit! Her hand hovered over a slim-cut, uncrushable blue evening dress that would be ideal for an impromptu social gathering. But would they be living in a tent or in one of the many forts he had told her were scattered throughout the desert? Did Arabs indulge in social functions, and if they did, would she be invited to attend or would she be condemned to segregation with the female members of the tribe? As the dress was so lacking in bulk, she finally decided to slip it into her case, together with a phial of her favourite perfume, before snapping shut the lid.

As the dress she was wearing was a simple shirt-waister in navy seersucker, crisp, cool, and ideal for travelling, she did not bother to change but sat down by the window to await Diego's pleasure.

Mere minutes had passed before he made a striding appearance. 'You are ready? Good!' he approved crisply, 'then come with me.'

With her heels beating a mad tattoo upon floors of blue azulejo tiles, she hurried in his wake, expecting to be led outside to a waiting car, but becoming more and more puzzled as they ascended stairs, crossed galleries, then finally emerged on to a flat roof towering high above the Castelo. The reason for their unusual mode of exit became apparent immediately she spotted the helicopter.

'Is that yours?' she exclaimed, taken aback by yet more evidence of undreamt-of wealth. 'It must have cost a fortune!'

'Just a small one.' For the first time Diego smiled, amused by her wide-eyed awe. 'In you get, little sparrow of the slums,' though his words were cruel his tone was kind, 'it is time you discovered the real thrill of flying.'

At first she sat tense, finding the appalling noise

and the vibration of whirling blades frightening,
but minutes after take-off fear gave way to the excitement of a totally new and wonderful experience
as she soared eagle-high above the Castelo, seeing it
slowly diminish to the size of a terra-cotta toy
perched on a miniature mountain.

Diego spoke little, but with his capable hands
on the controls he spared her several amused glances
as she craned her neck to peer down at the plain
below, entranced by her unique view of rich fruit
orchards, plantations of oranges and grapefruit,
quince, apple, pomegranate, pear and figs, of storks'
nests spread untidily beneath the crowns of immen-
sely tall trees, of colourful clumps of rhododen-
drons and bougainvillaea, masses of golden rod and
mimosa blossom, and then suddenly, unexpectedly,
a stretch of glorious deep blue sea.

*Portugal stands with its back to Spain, but with
its face towards Africa!* They had been flying only
long enough for Jade to become adjusted to the
sight of tiny ships ruffling the satin-smooth ocean
with creamy wakes, when Diego indicated an ap-
proaching coastline.

'Shortly we will be flying over Tangier towards
the mountains of the Rif, which is where we will
land.'

He seemed to understand her inability to make
conversation when the legendary, sinful Tangier
gave way to an exciting landscape dotted with
Moorish palaces sparkling like jewels in the clear
air inside which, she found it easy to imagine,
would be harems filled with concubines guarded by
eunuch slaves, and treasure houses piled high with
elephants' tusks, gold ornaments and jewels brought

across the Sahara by caravans of laden camels.

A glimpse of low hills with bare rocks cracked by the heat of the sun brought her partially back to earth, then the ground rose higher to form a range of black mountains pitted with canyons edged with low bushes ribboning the length of dry river beds. Gradually, the colour of the rocks began changing from brown to green, then a valley appeared beneath them, spread with hundreds of palm trees, their fronds shimmering in the haze.

'Do you see that ridge just above the point where two rivers meet?' Diego broke into her absorption.

'You mean the one with the Beau Geste fortress on its summit?' she questioned, peering keenly ahead.

'A very apt description,' he grinned. 'It was once a French fort and its one-time commandant, whom I visit regularly, has very kindly offered to accommodate us for the night. I advise you to make the most of your stay, *cara*, for it will be your last experience of civilised hospitality for some time.'

The commandant was waiting on the flat roof of the fort for the helicopter to land and immediately its blades stopped rotating he hastened towards Jade to help her down.

'Commandant Ruinart at your service, *madame*!' he saluted, then immediately unbent to direct a charming smile. 'But as your husband and I share a long-standing friendship, I would be both honoured and flattered if you would consent to call me Henri?'

'Of course I will, Henri,' she smiled, warmed by the friendliness of his greeting, 'and thank you for your offer of hospitality. My ... er ... husband has just told me that we are to stay here as your guests.'

Seemingly mesmerised by her sparkling, deep-green eyes, he held her gaze while he lifted her hand to his lips, but omitted to release it after kiss-ing her fingertips. As he stood gazing long and deeply at the creep of wild colour into her pale cheeks, Diego's amused drawl intruded.

'I did warn you, *mon ami*, to be prepared to meet my young and lovely bride—however, I should have known better than to have expected one of your incurably flirtatious nature to exclude any woman from your list of victims. Pay no attention to anything he says, *cara*,' he warned Jade, 'Henri is a born philanderer who woos only with words, is that not correct, my friend?'

'I flee all who chase me and chase all who flee me,' Henri admitted with a merry grin, 'but that is merely my way of playing for time. It is my belief that passion should strike root and gather strength before marriage is grafted on to it—I would not wish to win the hand of any woman unless I also won her heart. Unlike your lusty blood-brothers, Diego, I think it is as unjust to merely possess a woman as it is to possess a slave.'

Diego and Henri were each dark and upright, one as tall as the other, but there the similarity ended, for as Henri escorted her inside the fort she was struck by his chivalrous solicitude and by the gallantry she felt sure would be extended to every member of her sex whether old infirm, ugly or beautiful.

The interior of the fort was a revelation to Jade who had been expecting to discover the sort of spartan comfort that often accompanies a man

living on his own, but as they made their way down
from the rooftop a waiting Arab servant dressed in
spotless white was directed to show her to her room
while the two men continued downstairs to share
a drink and exchange news of mutual interest.

Her bedroom was luxuriously appointed, with
thick carpets underfoot and bright modern paint-
ings hung on smooth white walls. At each side of a
comfortable-looking double bed were lamps that
needed only the press of a switch to throw pools of
light upon the bed, and behind a connecting door
she discovered a tiled bathroom and modern taps
gushing out unlimited amounts of hot water. Obviously, Henri was no devotee of rough living; his
desert outpost was as comforably furnished as any
first-class hotel.

Feeling strangely lethargic, she lay down on the
bed for a nap, knowing she would not be missed
for at least a couple of hours by the two friends,
who met only infrequently and therefore had lots
to talk about. Shutters had been drawn across the
windows to keep out the worst heat of the sun, so
the room was cooled by shadows as Jade slipped
into a doze, blessing her foresight in packing the
evening dress she promised herself she would don
after a refreshing bath and long before the advent
of the dinner gong.

She awoke, however, to the sound of gushing
taps and movement coming from behind the closed
door. For a second she remained confused, until
her eyes lit upon a man's watch placed on one of
the bedside tables, upon a shirt flung across the
arm of a chair and underneath it a very familiar-
looking pair of shoes.

Diego was sharing her room!

At that precise moment the bathroom door was flung open and he emerged like an apparition from a cloud of steam, with a towel knotted around his lean middle, his tanned still-damp torso glistening like oiled silk.

'What ... what are you doing in here?' Jade jerked upright, her green eyes wide and startled.

'No need to react like an outraged virgin,' he replied coolly, picking up a comb to discipline his unruly hair, 'I'm your husband, remember, and Henri is a romantically-inclined Frenchman who automatically equates newly-weds with double beds. I could not find it in my heart to shatter his illusions by requesting separate rooms. Could you ...?'

It was not so much a question as a challenge, and as he swung round to face her she coloured, knowing he was waiting for her to choose between the embarrassment of trying to explain to Henri why she preferred to sleep alone and the even worse dilemma of having to share close proximity with the man whose magnetism could pierce even the shell around a frozen heart.

'I suppose,' she submitted stiffly, eyeing with alarm fingers fumbling with the knotted towel around his middle, 'I could always turn my back,' she finished in a hurry, turning her flaming face aside.

'Why bother?' he asked cheerfully, thoroughly enjoying her embarrassment. 'After all,' he pointed out a little more gently, 'we have already been as intimate as any man and woman can be. These hands of mine,' he sounded nearer, but she dared not turn round to see how near, 'have caressed

every inch of your delicious ivory beauty, and
once,'—no doubt now of the nearness of his mouth
to the nape of her slender neck, of his warm breath
playing tenderly upon her nerves—'you even for-
got your resentment long enough to kiss me in
return, right here!' His arm lashed her waist to
flick her round to face him, but she kept her eyes
closed, having no need to look at the spot he was
indicating, remembering only too well how rough
the crescent tattoo had felt beneath lips she had
pressed against his heart, how its barbaric presence had influenced tempestuous emotion to storm
her tense body, rendering it wanton.

The reminder brought a rush of revulsion, a
feeling almost akin to hatred of a man so insensitive
he could take moments of deep intimacy and use
them as barbs to pierce the composure that was her
only defence against his domination.

'Look at me, Jade!' His voice had developed
an edge. 'Only weeks ago you professed to love
me, so how can you remain so cold? Why must I
always take what a loving wife gives freely?'

She did look up then, showing eyes wide, green
and deeply accusing. 'I never loved you,' she told
him simply, bearing without a whimper his tightening grip upon her shoulder. 'I loved the tender,
considerate man I imagined you to be. You charged
me with deceit, Diego, but are you so guiltless in
that respect? Man is a moon with his dark side
hidden—it would seem,' she finished shakily, 'that
I'm condemned to live the rest of my life in your
dark shadow.'

It said much for Henri's expertise as a host that the

meal they shared that evening did not turn out to be a silent fiasco. Seemingly impervious to Diego's black-browed frowns of displeasure, he concentrated his attention upon Jade who, in her simple blue dress and with her pale hair brushed severely back and coiled into a chignon at the nape of her slender neck, reminded him of a pensive Madonna.

She was toying with a glass of wine, unaware that for some time he had been silently studying her perfect profile, when suddenly he startled her.

'Wake up, lovely dreamer!'

She jerked upright, almost spilling her wine. 'I beg your pardon, Henri, did you say something?'

He laughed aloud. 'I was merely urging you to forsake your fantasy world, *chérie*, but you have no need to look apologetic, it is our fault if you find your own thoughts more entertaining than your companions' conversation—or lack of it,' he amended, casting Diego a condemning look.

'I'm afraid,' she sighed, 'that since childhood I've been constantly warned against my tendency to escape into an imaginary world. I'm sorry ...'

'No need to be,' he frowned. 'To attempt to create an atmosphere in which all unpleasantness and pain are eliminated is really an act of self-survival. Obviously, *chérie*, at some time in your life you have been very badly hurt.'

'Perhaps,' she replied lightly, feeling the chill of Diego's eyes, 'but that was when I was a childish character who didn't want to grow up. Now that I'm more mature, I've learnt not to be so trusting.'

'My friend!' Henri's amazed eyes swung towards Diego, 'I trust that no action of yours has influenced such an amount of cynicism in one so young?'

Without waiting for a reply, he turned his attention back to Jade and continued, immune to the build-up of tension, 'As you have not yet been married long enough to find out for yourself, I feel it is my duty to help you to understand a little of your husband's complex nature. Diego is at heart a no-mad whose yearning for freedom has been frus-trated by his duty to maintain a permanent home and by heavy family responsibilities, consequently aggression builds up in him, an inner anger that cannot subside without the strenuous physical ac-tion for which his body is primed. That is why, periodically, he is forced to return to the desert, to what he regards as his native territory, where he can channel off his resentments by battling with nature and by enduring the hardships of an en-vironment that has remained unchanged for cen-turies. So you must not begrudge him his safety valve, *chérie*, for you, too, will be rewarded when the desert takes a tiger and returns a lamb.'

A quick glance at Diego's cynical mouth, brood-ing eyes and unyielding profile made the compari-son so ludicrous that in spite of herself she felt forced to smile.

'Ah! The rainbow after the storm!' Henri looked delighted. 'Come with me, *chérie*,' he rose from the table and held towards her a coaxing hand, 'I feel like dancing—and also I have an urge to make your unappreciative husband jealous.'

Diego rose to his feet, as politeness demanded, but seemed completely unconcerned about being left alone in the dining-room while Jade and Henri entered an adjoining salon with an uncarpeted floor ideal for dancing.

Predictably, Henri chose an album of sweet, romantic tunes, and as he turned from the record-player and held out his arms, she slid gratefully into them, feeling his solicitude as a feast after a famine of cool indifference. They were far enough from Diego to speak without being overheard, yet after dancing for a while in silence, Henri pulled her close to whisper against her ear.

'What has gone wrong between you two, *ma belle*? I've never known my friend Diego to be so dour and uncommunicative. And as for yourself,' his shoulders lifted in a shrug, 'I have known you mere hours, yet I sense that you wear your mantle of sadness not from choice but from circumstance. Should the cause be no more than a lovers' tiff, I shall not be offended if you tell me to mind my own business, but if it is something more serious and you need help, you only have to say so and you shall have it.'

'Thank you, Henri.' Her voice was husky with unshed tears. 'I appreciate your concern—nevertheless your first loyalty must be to Diego whose friendship I know you cherish.'

'More than cherish,' he admitted, his merry eyes grown sombre. 'We have shared much danger, Diego and I, and danger brings men closer than brothers. But I am not blind to his faults—he is proud as hell, intolerant of weakness, and like myself, has dined too often on the bachelors' fare of bread, cheese and kisses. Hunger does not breed kindness, Jade, indeed, it can be truthfully said that all vile acts are done to satisfy a hunger.'

Her wince of pain told him all he needed to know. For a while they danced in close communion, as he gave her time to decide whether or not to confide in him. He was disappointed, yet heartened by her loyalty to her husband when finally she prevaricated:

'You are so understanding, Henri, why have you never married?'

Accepting her decision without argument, he confessed wryly, 'Because I have yet to meet a woman willing to share my solitude. When Morocco gained independence and my job terminated I ought to have returned to France, but I had lived in this place for so many years, had become so attached to the land and its people, I found it impossible to pull up my roots, so I sold my estates in France and bought this fort which I had come to regard as my home. Unfortunately,' he sighed, 'one cannot also purchase a wife—or rather, I could,' he amused her, 'if I decided to settle for something less than love. Sadly, my taste does not incline in that direction.'

Suddenly he stopped dancing and with his arms linked loosely around her waist inclined his dark head closer to muse:

'How I envy Diego his good fortune, *ma belle*! If only I had met you first ...'

The grating of a stylus across the face of a record startled them apart. Diego, taut with leashed anger, was bending over the record-player reaching towards the control switch.

'Steady on, *mon ami*!' Henri protested mildly. 'Hereabouts, luxuries are in short supply, which is why we are careful to treat them kindly.'

'Remind me some time,' Diego spoke to Henri, but his angry eyes were upon Jade, 'to give you a lesson in the art of bribery. It has been said that the gods themselves are moved by gifts, and that gold does more to move men than words. Personally,' he grated, 'I've found that women seem to prefer pearls!'

With a tightness of control she found frightening, he beckoned imperiously to Jade. 'It's late, as we have to set off at dawn I think it would be advisable to retire now.' His steely eyes then swung towards Henri who, far from being disconcerted, was looking extremely complacent.

'Goodbye, Commandant.' His tone was caustic. 'Until we meet again I will try hard to remember that once we lived as brothers.'

CHAPTER TWELVE

THE next morning, just as the sun was rising, they left the fort in an old army truck borrowed from Henri. Jerrycans, some filled with water, some with petrol, rattled in the back as Diego drove along a rough track leading towards a belt of low hills, bare except for rocks making shadows cast by the rising sun.

The atmosphere inside the cab was suffocating even though a cool breeze was blowing through the open windows. Jade was bewildered by Diego's cold fury. Not a word had been exchanged between them since the night before when they had left Henri and gone upstairs together. Once inside the bedroom Diego's glowering menace had seemed to fill every corner, making her feel so nervous she had fled into the bathroom where, hampered by fumbling fingers, she had taken ages to undress.

Diego had been in a vengeful mood and past experience had proved the sort of punishment he favoured, so it had been with a dry mouth and a rapidly thumping heart that she had finally crept inside the darkened bedroom, only to be stunned at the sight of his tall form stretched out upon the floor with only a sheet as a covering and a flat pillow beneath his head.

She had dozed only fitfully, wondering about his amazing display of jealousy. He did not lack humour, yet in this instance he seemed totally un-

able to appreciate that Henri had set out deliberately to aggravate him, with a result that had far
exceeded expectation. Before sunrise, when he had
shaken her awake, she had seen from his grim
profile that his mood had not mellowed.

As the sun rose higher, poking long fingers of
light across the desert track she chanced a hopeful
sideways glance, but shivered and turned away from
a profile as austere as the night-chilled rocks strewn
around them.

An hour later, after topping a high rise, Diego
stopped the truck and relaxed to feast his eyes upon
miles and miles of solitary red-brown desert, completely devoid of vegetation, movement, sound or
smell—a vast impersonal void whose very emptiness
was frightening.

As if sensing her reaction, he derided her timidity. 'Are you feeling robbed of self-importance,
Miss High and Mighty?' She winced from the form
of address he used only when thoughts of her
deceit were uppermost. After drawing in a deep,
appreciative breath, he continued, 'Here in the
desert a man recognises his own insignificance, here
it is easy to understand why mystics find it easy
to meditate, to suppress their conceit, to subdue
the passions and desires of the body. Here a man
is but a lone speck of sand ...'

'Parched sand,' she dared to remind him, nervous of his new aura of vitality. It was as if one
breath of desert air had injected fire into his veins,
as if the radiance of the sun, the blue of the sky,
were reflected in his startling eyes. 'I'm thirsty,
could I please have a drink?'

'We'll do better than that, we'll have breakfast.'

Jade's heart lurched when she caught an unexpected glimpse of a smile as he reached inside the
back of the truck. 'Just coffee and sandwiches,' he
apologised, unscrewing the lid of a thermos flask.

'I don't mind,' she assured him, seizing eagerly
upon a packet of sandwiches.

'I somehow guessed that you would not,' he replied dryly, 'children love picnics and at times,
Jade, you display the reckless bravado of a wayward
child.'

Subdued by the censure, she munched in silence
food that had been rendered suddenly tasteless,
then unconsciously merited his rebuke by blurting
impulsively:

'You've no need to blame Henri for what happened last night. He was merely being facetious,
the last thing he intended was to cause a rift in
your friendship.'

The coldness of his eyes as they swung towards
her was like a douche of icy water upon her sun-
warmed cheeks.

'My friendship with Henri has endured greater
strains than any you could place upon it. How
could I blame Henri for falling into the same trap
I fell into myself? As I have already pointed out,
Jade, you are a dangerous combination of woman
and child, of glamour and naïveté—no man is
immune to wiles you have practised upon half the
male population of Lisbon, upon Henri, and even
upon Pedro, a simple-minded gardener's boy.'

He showed his savage contempt by tossing the
dregs of his coffee out of the window. For a moment
they lay a black stamp of anger on the sand, then
the moisture drained away, slowly and completely

as the blood had drained from Jade's heart.

Under a burning sun and cloudless sky, the truck bumped along its way until all sense of time disappeared, then eventually a tiny speck appeared and as they drew nearer she saw a man astride a camel, sitting motionless as a statue, his intent gaze fixed upon the distant horizon. Thinking he might have escaped Diego's notice, she pointed.

'Look, do you think that man has seen us?'

'Undoubtedly,' he replied dryly. 'He is a sentry whose duty it is to notice the approach of strangers long before they catch sight of him. The inhabitants of the desert have a highly-developed sense of sight, as well as an absolute immobility that helps to make them inconspicuous—an invaluable asset to men who are hunters, warriors and nomads.'

Almost immediately they passed the sentry the ground dipped and in a hollow, unseen and safe, sat women cooking food over fires built within a circle of black tents shaped like booths and divided into two parts by a hanging cloth. Obviously having been forewarned of their approach, men began pouring out of the tents heading in their direction and as Diego braked and stepped out of the truck dozens of voices roared a greeting.

'*Sheik Ana! Sheik Ana!*'

Seconds later they were surrounded by a horde of widely-grinning Arabs, tall, aristocratic men with fierce eyes and faces scorched almost black by sun and blown sand. The women, Jade noted with unease, remained in the background, groups of graceful girls with delicate, well-shaped hands, small feet, and a hint of beautifully curved limbs beneath loose, ankle-length garments.

An elderly Arab stepped towards Diego.

'Peace be unto you,' he blessed him, completely ignoring Jade.

'And to you be peace,' Diego replied gravely.

'You are well?'

'I am well. Thanks to God.'

With a great deal of back-slapping and talk in an unintelligible tongue, Diego was escorted into the camp by the male members of the tride, leaving Jade standing forlorn and deserted by the side of the truck. If his intention in bringing her here had been to humiliate, then he had more than succeeded—not even as an orphan in care had she suffered the same degree of insecurity, a lack of significance that made her feel less than the dust.

'Please, will you come with me ...?' Blinking tears from her eyes, Jade swung round in search of her questioner and saw a lovely young Arab girl with dark, soulful eyes. 'I am Mariam, fourth wife to Sheik Mamadou. Sheik Ana has asked me to see to your comfort.'

'How very thoughtful of him!' Jade almost choked on her indignation, then, realising that the girl's knowledge of English was sparse, she smiled her thanks and nodded, indicating that she should lead the way.

With graceful dignity the girl escorted her to a tent of a size and structure that set it apart from the rest. Stressing the fact that it belonged to a man of wealth and great status. Mariam indicated blankets spread out upon the floor of the interior.

'Faros,' she explained proudly, 'made of newly-born lambs' hides!'

A bashful child entered carrying a jug of milk

and a dishful of sugared dates, followed by a woman laden with a tray, teapot and kettle, sugar loaves, and a carton of green tea. Jade watched fascinated as she placed a handful of tea in the pot, poured boiling water over it, then tipped the liquid away. She then stripped the leaves from a sprig of mint and put it—stalks and all—into the teapot, together with a surprising amount of sugar, before pouring in more boiling water and then leaving the pot to stew. From time to time she sampled the brew until she was satisfied that the flavour was just right, then she poured out two glasses, one for Jade, the other for Mariam.

Politely, Mariam waited for Jade to take the first sip, but the glass was so hot she could barely hold it, much less transfer the scalding tea to her mouth.

'Let it cool awhile.' To Jade's relief Mariam took the glass from her agonised fingers and placed it on a low, brass-topped table. 'It is best drunk hot, but even when cool it can be very refreshing.'

Certain that she had wandered into some nightmare from which she would shortly waken, Jade tested her voice, hoping to accelerate the process.

'Where . . . where is my husband?'

'Sheik Ana—our leader—is in conference with the elders of the tribe,' Mariam told her simply. 'Though we had learnt of his recent marriage, his advice was needed urgently so we had to send for him. Sheik Ana never fails to come whenever he is called.'

'Your *leader* . . .!' The pitch of Jade's voice was shrill enough to have jerked awake the most profound sleeper.

'Certainly,' Mariam nodded, 'the most highly-respected member of our tribe. Only weeks before we heard of his marriage,' eyelids drooped over shy eyes, yet her admission echoed with natural simplicity, 'I was chosen to be his *moussa*, so to make up for my disappointment Sheik Mamadou took me as his fourth wife.'

'And what,' Jade asked faintly, 'is a *moussa*?'

'A temporary wife,' Mariam sounded surprised at her ignorance, 'a favour that is granted to all male visitors to our camp.'

Night had fallen by the time Diego deigned to seek her out. Flames from the campfires were leaping into the darkened sky, heating brazen pots in which mutton was seething in boiling butter and bubbling cauldrons of rice were being prepared for the feast that had been planned to welcome their leader.

The hanging cloth dividing the tent into two compartments was whipped aside and a tall shadow stooped to negotiate the doorway, then straightened immediately he stepped inside.

'You are honoured,' a drawling voice addressed her. 'As a great concession to me, the men have decided that you may eat with us.'

'Diego ...?' Her face was a picture of indecision, the voice was Diego's, but the figure dressed in a long black *seroual* and matching turban, with a dagger in a silver scabbard tucked into his belt, was pure Berber, a dark son of Satan!

'*Ou Allahi, inti zeyne hatt!* By Allah, how beautiful you are!'

Jade jumped to her feet, startled, yet angrier than she had ever felt in her life before. For hours he had left her to stew in a strange, frightening environment surrounded by the curious eyes of women some of whom had never seen a white girl before and had indicated that they were contemptuously unimpressed, had left her alone to brood upon the knowledge that upon each of his visits he enjoyed the favours of a *moussa*, a girl more than willing to act as stand-in for a wife. But she could not allow him to guess that the very thought of some other girl in his arms had sent a stab of red-hot jealousy tingling through her veins, had made her feel feline, wanting to claw at the beautiful Arab girl who had dared to covet her place. So she sought refuge in hauteur, a stubborn refusal to bow to his every whim.

'That is very kind of them,' she acceded stiffly, 'but I have no desire to share a meal with those men.'

With an animal grace of movement so swift it was shocking, Diego closed the space between them. She braced when his hands clamped down upon her shoulders, but was not prepared for a shaking so fiercely administered.

'You will do as I say or suffer the consequences,' he snapped with all the arrogance of a Berber lord. 'In the desert we have a strict code of etiquette in the matter of gifts:

'You must never refuse anything.

'You must never appear to expect the present received.

'You must never thank the giver.

'You must never forget to give something that appears valuable in the eyes of the Arab in return.

'Should you ever flout these rules your actions will reflect upon myself, and I would forfeit the respect I have earned as their friend and adviser. And now,' he stood with feet astride, arms folded across his chest, frowning down into her flushed, troubled face, 'will you dress by yourself, or must I help you?'

Noting a glint in his eyes that told her he found such a prospect pleasing, Jade abandoned all further argument.

'I can manage,' she told him stiffly. 'I'll be ready in half an hour.'

'You'll be ready in ten minutes,' he corrected smoothly. 'I'll stay here to make certain that you are.'

To spare her embarrassment he turned his back and pushed the tent flap aside to watch the activities of the camp while she fumbled her way out of the dress she had worn all day, splashed her face and neck with cool water, then slipped into a silver-grey skirt and matching blouse with long, full sleeves caught tightly at the wrists and a vee neckline deep enough to display the 'fig' amulet she wore constantly, the delicate ivory hand suspended upon a fine gold chain that was her only defence against the devil.

The subdued colour of her dress, only a few shades darker than her silver-pale hair, lent her a look of maturity that he was quick to notice.

'A baffling tranquillity shines out of your lovely eyes, *namorada*,' the low admission seemed torn from him, 'the sort of look with which a loving mother soothes a fractious child.'

His words revived the fiercest hurt of all, a hurt so deep she had pushed it to the back of her mind, willing herself never to brood, determined to forget that he had commanded her never to bear his child.

'You have already decided that that is one privilege I am to be denied,' she accused shakily, wide eyes dark with pain.

A shadow crossed his face as he stared down at the girl who, though he had made her his wife, still managed to carry virginal innocence like a shield. The silence was so intense his voice grated harsh as the heron, the night bird that winged through the darkness, earning the reputation of an evil spirit.

'Why do you want a child—are you hoping that, like most ferocious animals, I will be disarmed by the sight of my young?'

'No.' His mouth grew taut when she shuddered away from him. 'Motherhood must be wonderful, but I have no wish to be made even partly responsible for creating a life that might develop into a monster like yourself.'

The feast was laid out in the tent of Sheik Mamadou. After the ritual of brewing and drinking mint tea, two men appeared with a ewer and basin for the ceremonial washing of hands, then as they sat crouched upon the floor an enormous dish was placed before them containing a steaming stew of mutton, vegetables and spices.

'Try to eat only with the first three fingers of the right hand,' Diego instructed, helping himself from the communal dish. But to her inner disgust, Jade was forced to use both hands in order to manipulate even a tiny helping.

The first stew was followed by a second, pre-

pared with the same meat but with different spices,
but the *kus-kus*, steamed millet formed by hand
into small balls, then tossed into the mouth with
the aid of a dexterous thumb, defeated her utterly.
So she stuck to eating fruit and drinking glass
after glass of mint tea.

Shocked to the core by the men's lack of table
manners, by their gorging, and most of all by their
loud belching as they physically relieved the feeling
of repletion caused by gluttony, she begged in an
undertone:

'Please, Diego, let me go back to the tent!'

Unmoved by her threatened nausea, he nevertheless relented far enough to assure her, 'Any moment
now the men will retire to allow the women to
eat.'

As he inclined his head towards her, Sheik Mamadou looked up and boomed:

'You should force your wife to eat more, my
friend, she is too puny!'

'She will fatten with age,' Diego responded
calmly, but with a twitch of the lips Jade found
infuriating.

'She also looks sad—do you not please her in the
night?'

Feeling a heat of humiliation almost greater than
she could bear, she suffered Diego's casual glance
of appraisal, then wanted to curl up and die when
dryly he drawled, 'It is possible that she may be
feeling a little disappointed.'

The men fell about, guffawing with laughter at
this tremendous joke, their amusement accelerated
by the scandalised eyes and fiery cheeks of the
woman who, compared with their own buxom

wives, seemed more of a silver wraith.

'Oh, my droll friend!' Sheik Mamadou finally spluttered, holding his hands to his aching sides. 'I'd sooner believe my best stallion incapable of servicing a mare!'

Feeling this remark as the ultimate outrage, Jade jumped to her feet and ran from the tent, holding her hands over her ears to shut out the sound of men's laughter ringing loudly in the quiet night air.

No more than five minutes had elapsed when Diego joined her inside the tent. She was bending across a basin splashing shame-hot cheeks with water when she felt pressure upon her shoulder. She swung round, startled, and fell straight into the trap of his waiting arms.

'Jade,' he breathed, totally unrepentant, his warm lips seeking the curve of her mouth, 'don't be offended by the Arabs' earthy humour. They are not monsters, just lusty, virile men.'

'Who ignore women's very existence until they are in a mood for play!' she reacted like a she-cat, clawing her way out of his arms. 'Your friends *disgust* me,' she panted across a yard of space, 'and so do you! As you, too, seem to be in search of a plaything, *senhor*, I suggest you take advantage of your privileged position by accepting the services of a *moussa*!'

Immediately the words were uttered she realised that she had gone too far. The instant Diego had set foot upon the rolling sea of sand he had become as one with the desert and all its inhabitants, this land of Adam within which women did not dare to speak with contempt to men who hunted fiercely as tigers, who rode as swiftly and fearlessly as the wind.

Like a leaf in a sandstorm, she was lifted and twirled in a fierce pair of arms, then lowered, to lie trembling upon a bed of baby hides.

'A man has need of a *moussa* only in the absence of his wife, *querida*,' he murmured hoarsely, stabbing the darkness with eyes that were beacons of leaping blue flame. 'Hate me if you must, before this long night ends you will have time to warm to my passion, to cling, to urge, to beg me to love you—and to bitterly repent your attempted seduction of Henri.'

CHAPTER THIRTEEN

JADE limped inside her tent and hobbled across to a pile of cushions, annoyed by her own negligence in stepping barefoot outside. Mariam had warned her about the *initi*, coarse grass with seeds containing sharp poisonous little barbs which pierced the skin at the slightest contact, resulting in an unpleasant inflammation difficult to heal.

Rather than draw attention to her stupidity, she decided to doctor the wound herself, so she rummaged inside her handbag for tweezers and was relieved to discover also one small square of bandage. Carefully she probed for the barb embedded deeply into the sole of her foot and after a few agonising minutes succeeded in withdrawing the thorn from her flesh.

If only every thorn were as easily disposed of!

She sighed, her thoughts upon Diego who seemed to be becoming more and more Berberish with each passing day. Only yesterday she had forced herself to watch while, inside an arena of vociferous men, he had joined experts from the tribe to contest their skill in swordsmanship. Tense with horror, she had watched them twirling, fencing, jabbing, the air filled with bloodcurdling war whoops and slashing Damascus blades. She had closed her eyes, sickened by the violent spectacle, praying that Diego's swordsmanship was skilful enough to overcome his lack of a protective shield.

After carefully washing her foot and positioning the elastic dressing precisely over the puncture in her skin, she stood up to test her weight upon the injured foot and discovered that, though still smarting, it did not feel too uncomfortable. She had just finished clearing away when, for no concrete reason, she stiffened, sensing the presence of a husband who was swift to demand his dues yet who afterwards seemed bound to seek a couple of days' solitude in order to ease his conscience.

'*Bom dia, cara!*' She reacted with a jerk of fear to his mocking greeting. 'Today is market day at a nearby oasis, I have come to take you shopping.'

She spun round to protest, but a gasp caught in her throat at the shocking impact of brilliant eyes blazing above a scarf pulled across his mouth in the manner of the Berbers who believed that the face must be kept veiled in order to protect the soul.

'No!' she tilted shakily. 'I don't want your presents, what little I possess may be stolen but cannot be bought!'

'It was you who brought the spirit of the market-place into our relationship,' he reminded, striding angrily towards her. 'I had no wish for a marriage based on trade and barter, one that turned man and wife into seller and buyer!'

'A crooked buyer,' she choked, 'who thinks a pearl pin fair exchange for a broken heart.'

Her cringe when he reached out to grab her shoulders struck sparks from his cold eyes. 'The Arabs have a saying: Live together like brothers, but do business like strangers. That's all we are, Jade, strangers bound by the ties of marriage—

a wife who charges her husband a price for possession.'

The touch of his hands drew an agonised reaction from emotions he had breathed into life, from
nerves ultra-sensitive to hands that had set out to
punish but had digressed to a gentle chastisement
infinitely sweeter than pain. The reminder was gall
to her wounded pride; Diego was not a man who
would share, he wanted all or nothing, but however
much he might plunder there was one secret part
of her that could only be given—never stolen.

'There is a difference between what one takes
and what one really possesses,' she told him gravely.
'Touch a stray bird and you may kill it, keep your
distance and it may hop on to your hand.'

'... or fly away,' he concluded, blue eyes lazy.
'Sparrows, especially, are not easy to tame, *cara*,
therefore one is left with no alternative but to clip
their wings.'

He chose to travel by camel, holding her in
front of him as the huge, fearsome-looking beast
dipped and swayed across the sand-dunes with a
motion she imagined was very similar to that of
a ship plunging and breasting the waves. Less than
an hour after leaving the camp they began descending into a wide valley, a feast of green secreted
within a famine of sandy wasteland.

Her spirits rose as they drew nearer to fruit trees
and gardens and the sound of fresh water tinkling
from springs hidden in the palm groves. From every
direction people were making their way towards
the oasis, women carrying baskets full of green and
red peppers; charcoal vendors lugging heavy sacks;
a man shepherding a small flock of turkeys, and

richer merchants with donkeys laden with wares. Her nostrils flared to the smell of wood-smoke and roasting chestnuts, incense, jasmine blossom and rancid cooking oil, then a sound that had begun as a murmur in the distance developed into a deafening din of banging hammers, whirring potters' wheels, bleating rams, rasping saws and, above it all, the voices of hawkers peddling their wares and the ribald protests of incensed buyers haggling a price.

She winced when Diego lifted her from the saddle and set her down upon her feet.

'What's wrong?' he asked, his glance sharpening.

'Nothing,' she lied with forced serenity, 'just a slight touch of cramp, it will go off in a minute.'

'You're sure?' he frowned. 'People who aren't used to the desert must be extra careful of their health. The slightest ailment, the merest symptom, must be investigated and treated immediately.'

Not daring to admit that this often-repeated lecture had already been ignored, Jade insisted calmly, 'It's nothing, I assure you I'm perfectly well.'

They drew many curious glances as they sauntered the narrow alleyways of the *souk*, the tall, dignified Arab, obviously a Berber, but showing a puzzling deference to his slender female companion of a different culture and race.

Though her denim dress was modest and its skirt a respectable length she was conscious of glances being quickly averted from tapering ankles and shapely legs. Diego, however, remained unmoved by her blushing discomfort.

'You English say you are shocked when you are

merely embarrassed,' he chided coldly. 'You must be the coldest race on earth.'

An impulsive denial sprang to her lips, but was quickly swallowed back when she sensed that he was goading her into admitting that there had been times when he had forced from her responses as wildly passionate as his own ...

It was a relief when he guided her into a quiet alley out of earshot of tinny music being enthusiastically but badly produced from the flute, tambourines, lute and drum of a band of shuffling beggars. Stalls, small as pigeonholes, stretched the length of the jewellers' alley.

'The work of these crafsmen has been held in high esteem from time immemorial,' he informed her, pointing out a boy pumping bellows on to a pile of glowing embers. Next to him was a man working on an iron anvil. 'Even today, these people are the only ones capable of making the famous *dbailges*, filigree bracelets of beaten gold or silver. The skill of forging, riveting and polishing each individual piece is handed down from father to son.'

Jade could have watched the craftsman at work for hours, but as soon as he sensed their interest he stopped working to unlock a large iron-bound chest from which he began disgorging dozens of items of jewellery, offering them for sale.

'Choose whichever piece you wish,' Diego proffered a casual gift.

'No, thank you,' she declined stiffly, 'I already have more than enough jewellery.'

'These men are badly rewarded for their skill,' he rebuked her mildly. 'Would you deprive the jeweller's wife of a dress, his children of shoes?'

Forced into a corner, and with the jeweller's hopeful eyes upon her face, she could not refuse.

'Very well, if you insist, I'll take that one!' She pointed a finger without direction and it fell upon a bracelet, a simple, unembellished circlet of gold that she hated immediately Diego slipped it on to her wrist with the dry observation:

'A surprising choice—a band of bondage. It seems it must be true that slaves lose everything in their chains, even the desire to escape.'

They ate lunch in an eating house that had a spartan outlook, redeemed by a roof garden looking out over the green belt of palms, the shimmering desert, and in the far distance the shadowy peaks of a mountain range.

Jade was hungry enough to enjoy the loaves of barley bread, fresh butter and honey, but could manage nothing else but a glass of the inevitable mint tea which she sipped while Diego enjoyed his partridge *kus-kus*.

Noting her pensive expression, her air of solemnity, he queried, 'Now that you have had time to judge, what is your opinion of the desert and its people?'

She took time to consider. 'I find the desert majestic, austere, awe-inspiring, but I suspect that, like its menfolk, it can be very cruel, especially to what is laughably referred to as the weaker sex. From what I've seen, the life of the Bedouin women is one of ceaseless toil, it is they who spin the cloth to make tents, who cure goatskins to make buckets and water skins, who find fuel for the fires, who cook the meals and milk the goats—even when

they sit, their time is spent either spinning or rock-
ing skins on their knees to turn the butter. Yet the
men of the tribe seem to spend their days lounging
about drinking coffee and tea.'

'The women prefer it that way,' he told her
brusquely. 'To a Bedouin wife a husband is something of a sheik, absolute master of his own household, but contrary to the impression you seem to
have formed, his rule is not so much brutal as indifferent. The wives do not fight for attention, but
accept with good grace that they are inferior beings
and make up for their husbands' lack of interest by
indulging in ceaseless gossip and by tending to
their children—especially their sons, who are the
pride of their lives.'

'And you consider that fair?' She almost choked
on the indignation she felt on behalf of the ne-
glected wives. 'To be condemned to a life of ser-
vility, a beast of burden considered to be of less
importance than a camel in the eyes of her lord
and master?'

Her indignation deepened when she glimpsed
the suspicion of a smile ghosting across his lips,
before he rebuked her mildly:

'The men are not totally lacking in consideration.
As the amount of a wife's labour is so great he eases
her burden by taking three more.'

Now he was openly laughing, a wide grin creas-
ing cheeks contrasting brown as a nut against
startling white teeth.

But she was not amused. 'You're making fun
of me,' she accused huffily, pushing away her glass.
'I suppose that to you I'm just another empty-
headed chattel with no right to form an opinion,

much less state one! Has your close association with the Arabs coloured your outlook to the extent that you, too, would consider taking another three wives?'

Suddenly he was no longer laughing, his blue eyes grave as they regarded her steadily across the width of the table.

'If I did so, would you mind?'

Angered by the swift tide of jealousy her own suggestion had evoked, and by the effect his intense concentration was having upon her senses, she blurted:

'Good heavens, no! I should be grateful for the chance to become lost in the crowd.'

There seemed little point in lingering in the oasis; the atmosphere of truce that had grown gradually during the day had completely disappeared, leaving a yawning gap between them.

Nevertheless, as they wended their way back through the crowded market-place Jade felt an impulse to buy Diego a present. She told herself that the urge was born of pride, that it was simply a wish to discharge a debt imposed upon her by having had to accept his numerous and costly gifts, yet she searched scrupulously before making her choice, discarding items such as leather belts, pouches, tie-pins, medallions and wood-carvings until she found exactly the right thing—a small animal tableau carved out of ivory, a graceful gazelle in flight casting a stricken, terrified look across its shoulder at a pursuing panther. The gazelle was exquisite, but it was the panther that caught her attention because its creator had somehow managed to capture the feline grace of movement, the thrusting dominance, the supple body with its ripple of powerful muscles beneath silky skin that had become associated in her mind with Diego ...

When his attention was diverted, she seized the chance to exchange the pile of notes he had given her for the ivory carving, then managed to thrust it into her pocket just as he turned to find her.

'You have the look of a guilty child,' he frowned. 'Have you been sampling some of the sweetmeats I told you were forbidden?'

'Of course not!' She shuddered from the thought, the dust on the sweet vendors' stall supplying sufficient proof of lack of hygiene. Then in a stumbling rush she admitted, 'I've been buying you a present.'

'A present for me?' He looked so taken aback she was shamed into a wish that she had thought of it earlier. He had been so generous, yet she had not bought him so much as a wedding gift.

He grasped her elbow and guided her into a nearby palm grove, walking until the sound of the market-place had receded into the distance, then in a shaded spot cooled by the sound of running water, he turned her round to face him and requested quietly:

'May I see it?'

Nervously she dug her hand into her pocket and handed him the ivory carving. He held it in his palm and stared for long, silent seconds. Colour rose to her cheeks as she wondered if he would guess the line of thought that had prompted her purchase, but she felt inexplicably hurt when his harsh voice betrayed that he had placed upon the carving a totally different connotation.

'Is this how you see yourself, Jade, a timid innocent being pursued by a monster? Did you have to advertise your unhappiness in the only thing you have ever given to me of your own free will?'

When, without waiting for an answer, he bundled her out of the palm grove and made towards the tethered camel, she was overwhelmed by a lethargic sensation that was not entirely connected with the misery she felt at his misinterpretation. Her foot had grown uncomfortably tender, but she dared not limp, dared not admit that she had ignored all his cautionary lectures.

During the ride back to the camp she had to fight waves of nausea. Earlier in the day she had noted the camel's appalling smell, but on the return journey the stink of rancid sweat seemed to increase minute by minute until it reached the level of a noxious stench. It was as much as she could do not to scream when he lifted her from the saddle and set her down at the entrance to her tent. A red-hot needle of pain shot the length of her leg, then subsided to a pulsating throb.

'It was kind of you to take me to the oasis,' she thanked him politely as a schoolgirl after a treat.

'It is not like you to be sarcastic, Jade!' The shock of his terse reply jolted a surge of tears to her eyes. At the sight of them he frowned darkly. Pinching her chin between his finger and thumb, he held her face up to the sunlight.

'Perverse female!' he growled roughly. 'I have tried to meet the conditions of our bargain marriage, have heaped you with gifts, yet all you ever seem to do is weep.'

It was heaven just to relax upon cushions in the cool interior of her tent and to ease off the sandal from her rapidly-swelling foot. A wedding cere-

mony had been planned to take place that evening. All day the women of the tribe had been busy
preparing the bride, decorating her feet and hands
with henna and drawing lines resembling bright
yellow whiskers on her cheeks and down the bridge
of her nose. A special marriage tent had been erec-
ted, and she knew that Diego was expecting her to
join him to watch the wedding procession marching
three times around the tent before the men stormed
the entrance to break through the barrier of women
in attendance upon the bride.

'The bride strikes out with her slipper and if she
is successful in hitting the bridegroom it is supposed to imply that she will "wear the trousers",'
Diego had told her with a grin.

The ritual he had outlined had sounded so exciting and unusual she had been looking forward
to seeing it, but as she lowered her throbbing
head on to a pillow she knew that there was no
chance of her feeling fit enough to attend.

She slept for a couple of hours, but when she
awoke her headache was worse, the pain in her foot
agonising, her clothes soaked with perspiration.
Outside, the darkness was pierced by sparks from
flaring bonfires, the atmosphere throbbing with
the muffled beating of drums.

Even when Diego strode into her tent, handsome
as a Moor in a spotless white *seroual*, she did not
get up, could hardly muster a reply to his censorious
question:

'Aren't you ready yet?'

'I'm not coming, Diego, I'm so tired I feel I
must rest.'

'Of course you are coming!' he contradicted

brusquely. 'The wedding was put forward a few weeks simply for our benefit, and the bride and groom will be most offended if we do not attend.'

'You go,' she protested weakly.

'We will go together!' Fiercely he swooped to pluck her like a fledgling from her nest of cushions.

The pain when her foot jarred upon the ground jerked from her a cry of demented agony.

'Leave me alone! I hate you, Diego,' she sobbed, 'why, oh, why won't you let me go home!'

The thought of home was like a cool douche of sanity after a brainstorm, a blessedly uneventful heaven after a maelstrom of hell. The picture of Di's lovable, reassuring face was the last imprint upon her mind as she toppled in a dead faint, straight into his arms.

CHAPTER FOURTEEN

JADE'S return to consciousness was heralded by the sound of a bird sweetly singing. She lay with her eyes closed wondering why her limbs felt so weak, why her lethargy was so great she could not be bothered even to raise her eyelids. The perfume of jasmine drifted beneath her nostrils and as cautiously she curled her toes she felt the coolness of cotton sheets covering a comfortable bed.

Puzzlement teased her fuddled mind. Why had Mariam changed her *illiouich*, her white sheepskin bedcover, for the satin she could feel beneath her chin? Why was her bed so soft? And why was her mouth so dry, parched as the hot, dry desert? She ran the tip of her tongue around her lips and found them rough, cracked with lack of moisture. Then with what seemed to her a tremendous effort of will she attempted to call out Mariam's name to ask for a sip of water, of milk, or even some of her refreshing mint tea, but the only sound she managed was a sigh soft as the ripple of warm breeze through palm fronds.

And yet it evoked a response. She heard the creaking of a chair, a stirring of movement, then sensed a presence bending close.

'Jade ...?' The low, pleading voice was unrecognisable, its timbre was masculine, yet it could not be Diego's, for his voice was stormy, scathing, chilling—but never pleading. She had to see, had to

force her eyelids upwards even though they felt
heavy as a portcullis lain idle for years.

The sight of the face bending over her shocked
a feeble protest from her lips. 'Diego! You look
terrible, are you ill ...?'

Her languid green eyes deepened with puzzlement at his reaction—Diego, the Moorish lord,
with a wit sharp as steel, seemed at a complete loss
for words. He simply stared and stared with eyes
agitated as the Tagus in flood, his gaunt face made
piratically sinister by a dark growth of beard.

'No, *namorada*, I am not,' his low voice sounded
strained, 'but you have been very ill, in fact, there
was a time ...' As he broke off to swallow hard, she
suddenly remembered.

'Oh, yes, I had a headache and a sore foot ...!'

'But you did not tell me.' It was a flat statement,
yet she sensed a deep well of regret behind it.

'It was such a little thorn, Diego,' she struggled
to excuse her negligence.

'You are just a little thorn, *querida*,' he looked
surprisingly white and shaken, 'yet you were almost
my undoing. Don't talk any more just now,' he
dabbed her lips with something deliciously cool and
refreshing, 'go back to sleep. Once you have regained your strength we will resume our discus-
sion.'

There were so many questions she wanted to ask,
namely, why was she no longer in the desert? How
come she had been suddenly spirited back to her
room in the Castelo? But the heavy portcullis
began once more to press down upon her eyes and
she felt herself floating, but this time she did not

feel afraid—this time Diego had a tight, firm hold upon her hand.

Her first coherent thought when she awoke many hours later was that his hand was no longer holding hers. The realisation brought a sense of deprivation, a feeling that a lifeline had been severed, leaving her floundering. She dragged her eyelids upwards, searching for his face, but a stranger was bending over her bed, a young girl, obviously Portuguese, dressed in a nurse's white uniform.

'*Bom dia, senhora,*' the girl smiled, then bent to support her head, encouraging her to sip from a cup. It was plain that she could not speak English, for as she ministerd to her patient, bathing her face, neck and hands with cool, scented water, she communicated sympathy and understanding only with her dark eyes and ready smile.

Jade felt physically better, yet fretful, wondering where Diego had gone, why he had deserted her and left this pleasant, efficient, yet unknown stranger to take his place.

'Where is the Senhor?' The weakness of her voice surprised her.

'*Repouse, senhora,*' the young girl urged, shaking an admonishing finger. But Jade felt she had had sufficient sleep, her head was growing clearer by the minute and her foot felt completely painless. Only her heart was heavy, her eyes hungry for a sight of the man whose powerful presence injected strength into her veins.

For hours she lay waiting, timing the shifting rays of sun poking through the shutters and on to her bed, then gradually shifting across the floor and towards the walls, when she knew it was almost night time.

Afonso had surprised her with a visit. He had followed the nurse into her room, carrying a tray holding a bowl of soup and a vase crammed with glorious yellow roses. Solemnly he had set the tray down at the side of her bed, but instead of making his usual impassive retreat he had hesitated and indicated the flowers.

'These have been sent by the staff of the Castelo, *senhora*, as a token of our esteem and to convey our heartfelt wishes for your speedy recovery.'

'Oh, how lovely!' she had whispered, moved almost to tears. 'Please thank the servants for me, Afonso, and tell them how much I appreciate the kind thought ... and thank you, too,' she had added shyly, wondering whether the taciturn head of the household had meant himself to be included amongst the donors. From the very beginning Afonso had seemed to resent her presence, had spoken no words of welcome and though always scrupulously polite, his manner had been blatantly lacking in the sort of deference usually extended towards a new mistress.

His simple response had shaken her. 'We have all prayed for you, *senhora*—in a very short time, you have made yourself very dear to all of us.'

With the help of the nurse she managed to take a bath and afterwards, feeling greatly refreshed, she donned her prettiest nightdress and matching negligé, a floating peach-coloured ensemble trimmed with a deeper shade of lace and fastened at the neck and wrists with drawstring ribbons of peach-

coloured satin. Bed no longer appealed, so she sat in
a chair drawn up to the unshuttered window to
gaze out across the quickly darkening plain, hoping
for a glimpse of Diego riding his stallion towards
home, or driving his jeep from the direction of the
fields. But though she strained her eyes until night-
fall defeated her she saw no sign of him and
slumped back in her chair, too dejected even to
examine the reason behind the desperate need she
felt for the husband whose advances she had con-
tinually rejected.

His appearance was silent and sudden. One
minute she was alone in the darkened room and
the next he was making an approach, cat-quiet,
across the carpet.

'Do you enjoy sitting alone in the dark, *cara*?'
He flicked a switch and the subdued glow from a
bedside lamp suffused the small circle around them,
spotlighting his glistening, shower-damp hair; a
face tanned, smoothly-shaven, yet looking con-
siderably thinner, the profile finely drawn as if
sketched with a sharp-nibbed pen. He was dressed
for dinner and looked elegantly at ease, his shirt
front contrasting crisply white against the smooth
density of his jacket, his tie impeccably knotted,
diamond studs glinting discreetly from narrow-
edged cuffs.

'Nurse tells me that you are much improved,' he
bent to seek assurance from her face and seemed
satisfied by the colour creeping slowly beneath
creamy skin. 'Hmm, I see what she means,' he
frowned, 'yet you have such an air of fragility
still—as if the touch of a hand would break you
in two.'

Jade stifled an impulse to protest. All day she had waited, expecting to see signs of the same change of attitude she had undergone. For some inexplicable reason she felt they had shared a shattering experience that had drawn them so close there was no room left for misunderstandings. But the coolness of his manner, his casual, almost detached tone, brought the realisation that the tender arms she had sensed around her, the demented, loving whispers, the gentle fingers that had smoothed back her hair and stroked her brow, had been born of a fevered imagination, were all part of her own solitary dream.

She had to clench her fists and dig her fingernails hard into her palms so that she could remain calm when Diego drew up a chair beside her. He must never know how near she had been to throwing herself into his arms, must never guess how chilled and desolate she had suddenly begun to feel.

'I have some news that I hope will chase the shadows from your eyes, *namorada*,' he almost smiled as he bent towards her. But the smile was short-lived. Though his tone remained light, his expression was grave as he killed the last remaining hope she had nurtured. 'I have been in touch with your friend—the red-haired Di, who once tried to scrub away her freckles. She will be arriving here very soon to take you home.'

The impact of his words was shocking, yet somehow she struggled to retain a mask of composure behind which there was nothing but a stunned, empty void. Pride screamed to be redeemed, urging her to say anything to divert his attention from a mouth threatened by an uncontrollable quiver, so she latched on to the one part of his statement entirely unconnected with her agony.

'You and she must have had a long conversation,' she quavered. 'Di doesn't normally confess her childhood indiscretions to complete strangers.'

'Our telephone conversation was fairly short,' he confessed brusquely. 'She did not tell me—you did.'

'I did . . .?' Her wondering eyes looked enormous in a small, strained face.

For a moment he looked anxious. 'Are you sure you feel strong enough to be out of bed?' he asked sharply.

'Don't fuss, Diego,' she managed to pin a smile on to her lips, 'I can't recall mentioning Di's freckles, nor even the colour of her hair; are you certain it was I who told you?'

'Perfectly sure.' Her stunned nerves leapt into quivering life when he reached out to pluck her hand out of her lap and cradled it between hard brown fingers. Paying minute attention to her pink, unvarnished nails, he decided sombrely, 'I think it is about time that you were told exactly how ill you have been. This is not the time for me to scold, to berate you for your foolishness in neglecting to tell me about the injured foot that brought about such disastrous consequences, so I will content myself, for the moment,' his sharp glance promised later retribution, 'by outlining the effect of your negligence. Not surprisingly, the wound grew septic,' he continued, his jaw rigid, his eyes completely absorbed by the hand, slim and white as the ivory 'fig' amulet he had bought her, 'and you developed a raging fever. During your delirium you talked incessantly about your childhood, your adolescence, and mostly about your friend Di, your red-haired flatmate whose outspoken opinions often offended you yet to whom you still remained steadfastly loyal and devoted. It was not pleasant, listening to you babbling your innocent secrets, *cara*, but I am pleased you did so, because I think I now know almost as much about you as you know yourself.'

Jade stiffened and with a jerk regained possession of her hand. *Secrets*, he had said! Had she, in her delirium, allowed him insight into her innermost feelings? Had fever unlocked the door on the store of love she had determined would never be stolen if it could not be given freely? Had he discovered her secret, *and been embarrassed by it*?

The answer she sought was given when he rose to his feet to intone stonily, way above her head:

'Your last plea to me before you lost consciousness was that you be allowed to go home—the least I can do is to ensure that your request is granted.'

Long after he had left her she remained in her chair, dry-eyed and utterly defeated. When the nurse appeared to urge her into bed she lay down without argument, expecting to toss and turn the night away. But exhausion took its toll and she slept deeply, wakening the next morning feeling almost back to normal—a normality that included a heavily aching heart.

It was, as usual, a gloriously sunny day and as she gazed out of her window a glimpse of bright blue water gave her inspiration.

'I won't have breakfast just yet, thank you, Afronso,' she told the advancing manservant. 'Serve it by the side of the pool in about half an hour from now, I feel like a swim.'

The long pool lined with blue azulejo tiles was deserted. Cleanly, Jade dived into its cool depths and managed to swim one full length before her strokes began to weaken, warning that her bout of energy had been premature. She was gasping for breath by the time she reached the steps and clung gratefully to the arms reaching out to help her from the pool.

'*Enfant terrible!*' a voice exploded in her ear. 'Is there no end to your foolishness?'

'Henri!' She flung herself into the arms of the laughing Frenchman. 'I'm so pleased to see you, Henri, no one told me you were here!'

'No one cares,' he shrugged, pulling a towel around her shoulders. 'I'm tolerated only for my usefulness. Were it not that I could not bear to leave without assuring myself that you had quite recovered I would have returned to my fort days ago. At the moment, Diego is useless as a companion—every time I speak to him he growls back like a bear with a sore head. But enough of him, let's get you dried off, *chérie*, then when you are dressed perhaps we could have breakfast together?'

When, ten minutes later, she rejoined him at a table set upon a terrace overlooking the pool, she responded to his solicitude like a rose opening to the warmth of the sun, then after she had laughingly protesting that he was fussing too much, and assuring him that she felt completely well, he looked pleased and proceeded to enjoy his breakfast.

'I was intending today to ask permission to visit your sickroom to find out for myself how you were keeping.'

'Ask permission?' She stopped with a buttered roll halfway to her mouth to stare incredulously. 'But why should you do that? You could have visited me any time you wished.'

'Indeed I could not,' he exploded wrathfully. 'For the better part of a week no one has been allowed inside your room—not even your nurse! Diego insisted upon taking care of you himself, night and day he has watched over you, hardly leaving your bedside for a moment. But surely, *chérie*, he told you all this himself?' he exclaimed, puzzled by her stunned whiteness.

'No, he's told me hardly anything,' she admitted in a whisper, 'merely that I'd had a fever and been delirious—nothing more.'

'*Mon dieu!*' Henri's cup clattered into its saucer, 'what's wrong with you two, how can you ever hope to reach an understanding if you cannot, or will not, communicate?'

'*You* help me to understand, Henri!' she pleaded. 'Please tell me everything that's happened!'

Taking pity upon her bewilderment, he leant his elbows on the table and with his keen eyes watchful, proceeded to outline the events missing from her memory.

'The first I knew of your illness was when Diego arrived back at the fort, having driven across the desert, according to Mariam who was tending you in the back of the truck, like a man demented. You were, of course, at that time unconscious and running a high fever, but even so, I found his reaction puzzling and at the same time satisfying.

You see, *chérie*,' he digressed, 'although fever is nasty it is seldom in itself fatal, and Diego must have been perfectly well aware that you were in no danger from the poison in your foot.'

When she made as if to contradict, he waved her to silence and carried on implacably: 'Every tribe has its medicine man—witch doctor, if you like—but nevertheless, over the years Diego and I have both witnessed many miraculous recoveries achieved sometimes simply by the laying on of hands and at other times by the application of potions made up of ingredients known only to the medicine man. The point I am trying to make is this,' he leant closer, his expression deadly serious. 'Such treatments have never been known to fail. If either Diego or myself had to suffer a mishap similar to yours we would not hesitate to place ourselves in the hands of a medicine man, and yet although you had received such treatment, so far as Diego was concerned it was not enough. A decision was forced upon him. For years he has lived with a foot in either camp, not knowing quite where his true allegiance lay, but because he believed that your life was in danger he did not hesitate to spurn desert healing and rush you back to civilisation into the care of a qualified medical practitioner. So far as I am concerned,' he concluded triumphantly, 'that act proved the strength of his love for you. The least you can do, *chérie*, is to show him that you love him in return.'

Jade wanted desperately to believe him, but doubts preyed upon her mind, rendering her uncertain.

'How can I, Henri ...?' Her unhappy eyes begged for guidance.

'You are a young and ravishingly lovely woman, Jade,' he derided softly, 'do you *really* need me to answer that question?'

Thoughtfully, she left him and went up to her room, supposedly to rest, but for what was left of the morning and all during the afternoon she churned over in her mind all that Henri had said.

Diego loved her! Could she believe, *dared* she believe that by some miracle the love he had once felt had surfaced from beneath a sea of doubt and suspicion? But if he loved her why hadn't he told her so, why had he been in such a hurry to arrange her departure? Henri had implied that it was up to her to find out and instinct told her that he was right—even if the result was added heartbreak and embarrassment, she could not return to England with so many questions left unanswered.

Having decided upon a course of action, she fumbled her way into the simple evening dress she had worn when last she, Diego and Henri had dined together. Though feeling very much better, she still lacked sufficient energy to pay great attention to detail, so she applied the merest trace of make-up, and after brushing her hair, clipped it with a slide at the nape of her neck and left it loose.

Tension built up inside her as she waited for a sign of Diego's return, so that when she recognised the sound of movement coming from the adjoining room she began trembling so violently she had to pause and draw in a deep, steadying breath before knocking on the door.

'*Entrez!*' His tone was so enquiring she had to force herself to step inside his room.

'Jade!' He strode to meet her. 'What's wrong? You're very pale.'

'Nothing is wrong,' she stammered painfully, wondering what had possessed her to impose her presence upon the stern-faced *fidalgo* who looked too self-possessed, too coldly aloof to lose his heart to any woman, much less her insignificant self. 'I ... want to talk to you.'

His eyebrows drew together in a frown. 'You should be resting. I'm not convinced that you are well enough to talk to anyone just yet, but as you look so upset perhaps you had better tell me what is worrying you.'

But when the moment of decision was upon her she dried up, could not think of a single word to say. He was dressed ready to go downstairs, probably intending to join Henri for a drink before dinner, and as she floundered, praying for inspiration, his look of impatience swept a wave of colour into her cheeks.

'Henri seems to think ...' she began. 'I was hoping ...'

'Yes, Jade?' he prompted, as if feeling forced to humour her. 'What is it that you are hoping?'

'Diego, do I have to leave?' she jerked suddenly. 'Do you really want me to go away?'

His stark reply drained her of every vestige of colour. 'Yes, Jade,' he turned his back and strode across to the window, 'I want you to go home.'

'But why?' she gasped, then, fired by a sudden determination to discover the truth, however painful, she insisted, 'Less than a week ago you vowed that we would always remain together, when I pleaded with you to allow me to spend a holiday in England you insisted I had to stay, yet now ...' she faltered.

'Now I have changed my mind,' he concluded, his voice implacable, unbending as his rigid frame. 'At that time I meant what I said, but that was before you became ill, before I realised how badly I had misjudged you, before I learned how much you had been made to suffer on account of my insufferable pride.'

'Diego,' she pleaded, feeling a faint stirring of hope, 'your reaction to my imagined deceit was perfectly understandable—and anyway, I was mostly to blame.'

'How can you be blamed for *my* cruelty,' he spun round to challenge harshly, 'my stupidity in taking you into territory to which you were totally unsuited? *Meu Deus*, Jade,' he jerked violently, 'don't you realise that it was because of my negligence that you almost died?'

He was so full of inner anger, so determined to carry out his own crucifixion, she saw that nothing she could say or do would make him change his mind. For long appalled seconds she stared into his tortured eyes, then feeling absolute despair she cried, 'I wish I had, I'd rather be dead than have nothing to live for, no one who cares about me. I think, Diego,' she bit sharply into a quivering lip, 'that I must have been born to lose. Everything and everyone that I've ever cared about has been taken from me—my mother, my home, my friends, and now you have taken my love, my dreams, my heart, and left me with nothing. Do you wonder that I'm sick of playing this game of life when I'm always the loser?' Unable any longer to quell the tears that never failed to goad him into anger, she ran blindly from the room, along passageways, down stairs, neither knowing nor caring in which direction she was heading.

It was still light, but the gardens were deserted when she ran outside, blinded by hot tears of misery that were stinging her cheeks and burning behind her eyes. When the small rose-covered arbour loomed she ran inside, flung herself into a chair and with her arms spread out upon the table lowered her head and abandoned herself to heart-break.

Lost in a storm of tears, she did not hear Diego speak her name, so was shocked into silence when he pulled her to her feet and into his arms.

'No more tears, *namorada*,' he begged thickly. 'I cannot bear to see you cry.' When her lips parted in wonderment he sealed them with a kiss that communicated love, desire, and passionate need, without the use of one word.

Bemused with happiness, she responded with an eager passion that forced him to crush her so close her slender body merged with his.

'*Meu amor*, I adore you, precious Jade, how could I possibly have continued trying to be noble when your sweetness was driving me insane?'

She was given no time to question, to wonder at this miracle, before being swept off her feet and swung high into his arms.

'What are you going to do, Diego?' she murmured, too deliriously bemused to really care.

'I am going to make love to my wife,' he promised

hoarsely, burying his lips in her hair, 'and this time my wife is going to make love to me in return. *Isn't she*, Jade ...?'

He waited, eyes intensely blue compelling her to answer.

'Oh, yes, my darling,' she nodded solemnly, displaying the whole of her gentle, loving heart in her eyes, 'this time she most certainly will!'

Harlequin Plus

A WORD ABOUT THE AUTHOR

Margaret Rome's first Harlequin was published in 1969. Appropriately, it was entitled *A Chance to Win* (Harlequin Romance #1307).

But her chance was a while in coming. In her teens Margaret dealt with a long-term bout of rheumatic fever; then followed a series of manual jobs that "just could not satisfy my active mind," and finally marriage and the birth of a son. But at last, when Margaret did get down to the business of writing—beginning by doodling with pen and paper—she discovered that a sentence formed, a second one followed, and before long, paragraphs had developed into a chapter. "I had begun the first of many journeys," she says.

Today Margaret and her husband make their home in Northern England. For recreation they enjoy an occasional night out dancing, and on weekends they drive into the beautiful Lake District and embark on long, invigorating walks.

What readers say about Harlequin romance fiction...

"Harlequin romances give me a whole new outlook on life."

"Thank you so much for all those lovely hours of entertainment."

"Harlequin is the best in romantic reading."

"Thank you very much for letting me subscribe to Harlequin romances."

"A pleasant way to relax after a busy day."

*Names available on request.

FREE!

A hardcover Romance Treasury volume
containing 3 treasured works of romance
by 3 outstanding Harlequin authors...

...as your introduction to Harlequin's
Romance Treasury subscription plan!

Romance Treasury

...almost 600 pages of exciting romance reading
every month at the low cost of $6.97 a volume!

A wonderful way to collect many of Harlequin's most beautiful love
stories, all originally published in the late '60s and early '70s.
Each value-packed volume, bound in a distinctive gold-embossed
leatherette case and wrapped in a colorfully illustrated dust jacket,
contains...
• 3 full-length novels by 3 world-famous authors of romance fiction
• a unique illustration for every novel
• the elegant touch of a delicate bound-in ribbon bookmark...
  and much, much more!

Romance Treasury

...for a library of romance you'll treasure forever!

Complete and mail today the FREE gift certificate and subscription
reservation on the following page.